William Shakespeare's The Taming of the Shrew: A Retelling in Prose

David Bruce

Published by David Bruce, 2022.

WILLIAM SHAKESPEARE'S THE TAMING OF THE SHREW: A RETELLING IN PROSE

First edition. July 28, 2022.

Copyright © 2022 David Bruce.

ISBN: 979-8201368241

Written by David Bruce.

Table of Contents

Dedication

Dedicated to My Uncle Reuben Saturday

When he was a young man, my mother's brother Reuben wanted to escape from poverty and lard sandwiches, so he tried to run away from it. He stole a car so he could drive up north where he hoped to find opportunity, but he got caught and ended up on a Georgia chain gang for several months. In a chain gang, prisoners are shackled every few feet by the ankles to a long length of chain to keep them from escaping. They work in the hot sun while shackled to the chain, and when they sleep, they are shackled to the bed. No freedom, hard work, hot sun, no pay, bad food, and some mean guards.

When my uncle got released from the chain gang, he hitchhiked up north. He did what a lot of people trying to escape from poverty do: He drifted. He drifted from town to town, seeking opportunity and not finding it. He worked when he could, but the jobs were temporary and low pay. My uncle slept rough often, and he was hungry often. Once, when he was completely broke and completely hungry, he saw a restaurant with a buffet and went inside and asked to speak to the manager. He said, "I am very hungry, I don't have any money, and I would appreciate it very much if you would give me any food that the restaurant is going to throw away. I will be happy to wait by the rear entrance until you are ready to throw away food."

The manager told him to sit down at a table, and then the manager went to the buffet, loaded a big plate high with food, and gave it to him free of charge.

One way out of poverty is to get a good job, and my uncle got out of poverty by getting a job working with sheet metal.

My uncle's work ethic helped him. His employer sent him to California to do some special sheet-metal work, and the people in California wanted to keep him there. They explained that their California employees liked to come to work late, leave early, and take many days off. It was difficult to get someone who would show up and do the work they were supposed to do and were paid to do.

My uncle was also good with money. He got married, bought a house, and raised six children. Each time he made a mortgage payment, he paid extra money so he could pay off the mortgage faster.

If there was a sale on food, he bought lots of it. For example, if there was a sale on peanut butter, two jars for the price of one, he would buy twelve jars and sometimes go back the next day and buy six more jars.

If you went in his pantry — a closet set aside to store food — you saw that it was packed with food. If you went in his kitchen, you saw that he had taken off the doors of the high cabinets in which he stored food so that he could see the food. If you went in his bedroom, you saw that he had all the regular bedroom furniture, but he also had lots of shelves he had installed. The shelves were loaded with things that he had bought on sale that he knew his family could use: food (of course), light bulbs, toothpaste, toilet paper, etc. His bedroom looked like a warehouse.

Once he made a bad purchase: he bought a case of baked beans. Beans are beans, but the sauce they came in can taste good or bad, and the sauce these beans came in tasted bad. His kids told him, "Dad, throw those beans away! They're awful!"

But when you grow up poor, you don't throw beans away. For a long time, whenever my uncle and his family ate baked beans, they ate a mixture of one can of good baked beans and one can of bad baked beans.

My uncle's kids never had to eat lard sandwiches.

***

The doing of good deeds is important. As a free person, you can choose to live your life as a good person or as a bad person. To be a good person, do good deeds. To be a bad person, do bad deeds. If you do good deeds, you will become good. If you do bad deeds, you will become bad. To become the person you want to be, act as if you already are that kind of person. Each of us chooses what kind of person we will become. To become a good person, do the things a good person does. To become a bad person, do the things a bad person does. The opportunity to take action to become the kind of person you want to be is yours.

Educate Yourself
Read Like A Wolf Eats
Be Excellent to Each Other
Books Then, Books Now, Books Forever

***

In this retelling, as in all my retellings, I have tried to make the work of literature accessible to modern readers who may lack some of the knowledge about mythology, religion, and history that the literary work's contemporary audience had.

Do you know a language other than English? If you do, I give you permission to translate this book, copyright your translation, publish or self-publish it, and keep all the royalties for yourself. (Do give me credit, of course, for the original retelling.)

I would like to see my retellings of classic literature used in schools, so I give permission to the country of Finland (and all other countries) to give copies of this book to all students forever. I also give permission to the state of Texas (and all other states) to give copies of this book to all students forever. I also give permission to all teachers to give copies of this book to all students forever.

Teachers need not actually teach my retellings. Teachers are welcome to give students copies of my eBooks as background material. For example, if they are teaching Homer's *Iliad* and *Odyssey*, teachers are welcome to give students copies of my *Virgil's* Aeneid: *A Retelling in Prose* and tell students, "Here's another ancient epic you may want to read in your spare time."

CAST OF CHARACTERS

A Lord.

CHRISTOPHER SLY, a Tinker.

Other persons in the Introduction: Hostess, Page, Players, Huntsmen, and Servants.

BAPTISTA, a rich Gentleman of Padua.

VINCENTIO, an old Gentleman of Pisa.

LUCENTIO, son to Vincentio; in love with Bianca. Lucentio pretends to be a tutor named Cambio.

PETRUCHIO, a Gentleman of Verona; Suitor to Katharina.

GREMIO, HORTENSIO, Suitors to Bianca. Hortensio pretends to be a tutor named Litio.

TRANIO, BIONDELLO, Servants to Lucentio. Tranio pretends to be Lucentio.

GRUMIO, CURTIS, Servants to Petruchio.

PEDANT, an old man, set up to impersonate Vincentio.

KATHARINA, the Shrew, and BIANCA, Daughters to Baptista.

Widow.

Tailor, Haberdasher, and Servants attending on Baptista and Petruchio.

SCENE: Padua, Italy, and Petruchio's country house.

INTRODUCTION
Part 1

Tinkers — repairers of pots and pans — have a reputation for drinking way too much, and Christopher Sly lived up to that reputation. Right now, he was drunk and being thrown out of an alehouse because he had broken so many glasses. The arguing between Christopher Sly and the hostess of the inn had carried them a little distance from the alehouse. They were now on a heath that belonged to a Lord — they were near the Lord's house.

"I'll get even with you," Christopher Sly threatened the hostess of the inn.

"And I'll get a pair of stocks for you," the hostess threatened back.

A pair of stocks was used to punish criminals. Their feet would be put in holes in wooden beams. Once their feet were secured, the criminals could not run away. If a crowd of people were angry at the criminal, they would torment the criminal.

"You are a baggage — a loose and good-for-nothing woman," Christopher Sly replied. "The Slys are no rogues; look in the historical chronicles; we came in with Richard the Conqueror."

The Hostess thought, *He means William the Conqueror, but since he got the name wrong, he is probably lying about his family's historical importance.*

Christopher Sly continued, "Therefore *paucas pallabris* — I know my Spanish for 'few words' — let the world pass. *Sessa!* — I know my Spanish for 'cease!' 'scram!' and 'shut up!'"

"You will not pay for the glasses you have broken?" the hostess asked him.

"No, not a denier — not a penny. Here's a quotation from Thomas Kyd's *The Spanish Tragedy*: 'Go by, Jeronimy.' Beware, Jeronimy."

The Hostess thought, *It is an inaccurate quote. The character's name in the play is Hieronimo, but this drunken tinker has mixed the name up with the name of Saint Jerome, aka Hieronymus.*

Christopher Sly added an insult for the Hostess, "Go to your cold bed, and do something that will warm you."

"I know the remedy for my problem," the Hostess said. "I must go and fetch the third borough — the constable."

The Hostess left to fetch a constable.

"The third, or fourth, or fifth borough, I'll answer him according to the law," Christopher Sly said. "I'll not budge an inch, wretch. Let him come, and welcome."

A hunting horn soon sounded, and a Lord and his men came over to Christopher Sly, who had fallen asleep.

The Lord said, "Huntsman, I order you to take good care of my hounds. Let Merriman breathe and recover his breath; the poor hunting dog is foaming at the mouth. And couple Clowder with the deep-mouthed bitch. Did you see how Silver picked up the scent at the corner of the hedge when it was faintest? I would not lose the dog for twenty pounds."

The first huntsman said, "Why, Bellman is as good as he, my Lord. He discovered the scent and cried out twice when it seemed completely lost. Trust me, I take him for the better dog."

"You are a fool," the Lord said. "If Echo were as fast, I would esteem him worth a dozen dogs such as Bellman. But feed them well and look after them all. Tomorrow I intend to hunt again."

"I will, my Lord."

Seeing Christopher Sly, the Lord said, "Who is here? One dead, or drunk? Look and see whether he breathes."

The second huntsman said, "He breathes, my Lord. Were he not warmed with ale, this would be a cold bed in which to sleep so soundly."

"Oh, monstrous beast! How like a swine he lies!" the Lord said. "Grim death, how foul and loathsome is your image! Sleep is the counterfeit of death. Sirs, I will play a joke on this drunken man. What do you think — if he were carried to a bed and wrapped in fine and scented clothes, rings put upon his fingers, a most delicious light meal placed by his bed, and finely dressed attendants located near him when he wakes, wouldn't the beggar then forget who he is? Wouldn't he think that he is a Lord and not a beggar?"

"Believe me, Lord," the first huntsman said. "I think he could not believe anything other than that he is a Lord."

"Everything would seem strange to him when he awoke," the second huntsman said.

"It would seem to him like a flattering dream or flight of imagination," the Lord said. "Pick him up and carry out the jest well. Carry him gently to my best bedchamber and hang in it all my tapestries depicting amorous scenes. Bathe his foul head in warm rosewater made from distilled rose petals, and burn sweet wood such as juniper or pinecones to make the lodging smell good. Make sure that music is ready to play when he wakes — let the music make a melodious and a Heavenly sound. If he happens to speak, be ready to immediately and with a low submissive bow say, 'What is it your honor will command?' Let a servant attend him with a silver basin full of rosewater and bestrewed with flowers. Let another servant bear a ewer — a large jug with a wide mouth. Let yet another servant bring a towel and say, 'Will it please your Lordship to cool your hands?' Let a servant be ready with an expensive suit of clothing and ask him what apparel he will wear. Another servant will tell him of his hounds and horses, and that his lady mourns because of his disease. Persuade him that he has been insane, and when he says he is out of his mind now, say that he is mistaken, for he is in fact a mighty Lord. Do these things and do them convincingly, gentle sirs. It will be an extremely excellent practical joke if we do things properly and without overdoing them."

"My Lord, I promise you that we will play our parts well," the first huntsman said, "and because we will skillfully and diligently play our parts he shall think he is no less than what we tell him he is: a Lord."

"Pick him up gently and take him to bed," the Lord said. "Each one be ready to perform his part when he wakes up."

Some huntsmen carried out Christopher Sly as a trumpet sounded.

The Lord said to a servant, "Go and see what trumpet it is that sounds."

A servant exited to carry out the order.

The Lord said, "Probably, the trumpet announces that some traveling noble gentleman intends to stay here tonight."

The servant came back, and the Lord asked, "Who is it?"

"Sir, it is a group of actors who are offering their services to your Lordship. If you are willing, they will perform a play for you."

"Tell them to come here."

The actors came over to the Lord, who said to them, "Fellows, you are welcome here."

"Thank you," the actors replied.

"Do you intend to lodge with me tonight?"

"If it pleases your Lordship," an actor replied.

"It does, with all my heart," the Lord said.

He looked at an actor and said, "This fellow I remember. I once saw him play a farmer's eldest son. It was where you wooed the gentlewoman so well. I have forgotten the name of the character, but I remember that you were well suited for that part and performed it well and realistically."

The player replied, "I think it was the role of Soto that your honor means."

"Yes, that was it," the Lord said. "You performed the role excellently."

The Lord said to all the actors, "Well, you have come to me at a good time because I require some entertainment and your talents can assist me much. A Lord will hear your play tonight. But you must be capable of self-control. This Lord has never seen a play and he may behave oddly. I am afraid that if you pay too much attention to his odd behavior that you will begin to laugh at him and thereby offend him. I must tell you that if you even smile at him he will grow irritable."

An actor replied, "Fear not, my Lord. We can control ourselves even if he is the most eccentric and oddest man in the world."

The Lord ordered a servant, "Take these actors to the buttery — the liquor pantry — and give all of them a friendly welcome. Let them lack nothing that my house can offer."

The servant and the actors exited.

The Lord ordered another servant, "You go to Bartholomew, my young page, and tell him to dress himself up like a lady. Once that is done, take him to the drunkard's bedchamber, and call Bartholomew 'madam' and pay him respect. Tell him from me that if he wants to earn my gratitude, he will behave in a dignified manner such as he has observed that noble ladies behave toward their husbands. Let him pretend to be the drunkard's wife and act that way toward him. Let Bartholomew speak softly to the drunkard with humble courtesy and say, 'What is it your honor will command, wherein your lady and your humble wife may show her duty to you and make known her love for you?' And then with kind hugs, tempting kisses, and with her — that is, his — head lying on the drunkard's chest, tell Bartholomew to shed tears, overjoyed to see her noble Lord restored to health, who for the past seven years has thought himself to be no better than a poor and loathsome beggar. If the boy Bartholomew does not have not a woman's gift to rain a shower of tears at will, an onion will do well to cause such tears. An onion in a handkerchief being secretly conveyed to his eyes will make his eyes water and overflow with tears. See that this is done as quickly as you can. Soon I will give you more instructions."

The servant exited.

The Lord said to himself, "I know the boy Bartholomew will well assume the grace, voice, walk, and bodily movement of a gentlewoman. I long to hear him call the drunkard 'husband.' I long to see how my men will stop themselves from laughing when they show respect to this simple peasant. I will go inside to give them their instructions. Perhaps my presence will dampen their over-merry spirits that could easily grow into extremes."

Part 2

Christopher Sly was lying on a bed in the Lord's bedchamber. Around him were many servants. Some servants held fine clothing. Other servants held such items as a basin and a ewer. The Lord was also present.

Christopher Sly yelled, "For God's sake, bring me a pot of small — weak and diluted — ale."

The first servant asked, "Will it please your Lordship to drink a cup of imported sack?"

The second servant asked, "Will it please your Honor to taste this fruit preserved in sugar?"

The third servant asked, "What clothing will your Honor wear today?"

"I am Christophero Sly," he responded, using a Spanish version of his name. "Do not call me 'Honor' or 'Lordship.' I have never drunk sack in my life — imported wine is too expensive for the likes of me and if you give me anything preserved in something else, then give me beef preserved in salt. Never ask me what clothing I will wear; for I have no more jackets than I have backs, no more stockings than I have legs, and no more shoes than I have feet. In fact, sometimes I have more feet than I have shoes, and sometimes when I do have shoes, my toes can be seen even when I am wearing the shoes."

The Lord said, "May Heaven stop this foolish, absurd mood of yours! It is a pity that a mighty man of such descent, with such great possessions and held in so high esteem, should be infected with so foul an illness!"

"What, would you make me mad? Am not I Christopher Sly, old Sly's son of Burton-heath, which is near Stratford-upon-Avon, by birth a peddler, by education a cardmaker who makes combs for working with wool? Have I not had a job as a keeper of a trained bear, and am I not now by present profession a tinker? Ask Marian Hacket, the fat wife of a keeper of an alehouse in Wincot, which is also near Stratford-upon-Avon, about me — ask her whether she knows me. If she does not say that I owe her fourteen pence on my tab just for ale, call me the lyingest knave in Christendom. Listen to me! I am not out of my mind. Here's —"

The third servant interrupted, "This is what makes your wife mourn!"

The second servant said, "This is what makes your servants hang their heads and feel sorrow for you!"

The Lord said, "This is why your relatives shun your house — it is as if your strange lunacy beats them away from your door. Oh, noble Lord, remember your birth. Call your former reason and original sanity home from banishment and banish from yourself these abject lowly dreams. Look how your servants serve you — each servant is ready to do your bidding. Do you want to hear music? Listen. Apollo, the god of music, plays for you."

Music began to play.

The Lord continued, "And twenty caged nightingales sing for you. Or do you prefer to sleep? We will have for you a couch made up that is softer and more perfumed than the bed made up for Semiramis, the Assyrian Queen who was famous for her sexual appetite. Do you wish to walk? We will spread rushes before you to walk on. Do you wish to ride on horseback? Your horses shall be draped in decorative coverings and their harnesses studded and decorated with gold and pearls. Do you wish to go hawking? You own hawks that will soar above the morning larks. Or do you wish to hunt? Your hounds shall make the welkin — the sky — answer their cries. Shrill echoes will come from the depths of the earth."

The first servant said, "If you wish to hunt hares, your greyhounds are as swift as rested stags — indeed, they are fleeter than the young deer."

The second servant said, "Do you wish to look at pictures? We will immediately fetch for you a painting of Adonis by a running brook and Venus, who loved him, hidden among rushes that seem to play amorously as they are moved by her sighs as she spies on him. The rushes move with her breath just like they move when wind blows over them."

The Lord said, "If you want us to, we will show you a painting of Io when she was a maiden and Jupiter tricked her and visited her to make love to her. Afterward, Jupiter's wife, Juno, changed Io into a cow. This painting is very realistic."

The third servant said, "Or we will show you a painting of Daphne fleeing from Apollo in a thorny wood — the thorns scratch her legs and she cries. This painting is done so realistically that you shall swear she bleeds. Even the god Apollo would weep at that sad sight because the blood and tears are painted so skillfully."

"You are a Lord, and nothing but a Lord," the Lord said to Christopher Sly. "You have a wife who is far more beautiful than any other woman in this corrupt and declining age."

The first servant said, "Until the tears that she has shed for you flowed over her lovely face like malicious floods, she was the most beautiful woman in the world. Even now, she is inferior to none."

The mention of a wife — a bed-partner — interested Christopher Sly, who said, "Am I a Lord? And have I such a wife? Do I dream? Or have I dreamed until now? I do not sleep: I see, I hear, I speak; I smell sweet fragrances and I feel soft things. Upon my life, I am a Lord indeed. I am not a tinker, and I am not Christophero Sly. Well, bring my wife here before me. And, as I said before, bring me a pot of the smallest ale."

The second servant said, "Will it please your mightiness to wash your hands? Oh, how we rejoice to see your sanity and wit restored! Oh, that once more you knew but what you are! These fifteen years you have been in a dream. Even when you were awake, it was as if you slept."

"These fifteen years!" Christopher Sly said. "By God, that is quite a nap. But didn't I ever speak in all that time?"

The first servant replied, "Oh, yes, my Lord, but you spoke very silly words. Although you lay here in this fine bedchamber, yet you would say that you were being beaten out of a tavern. And you would shout about the hostess of the tavern and say that you would take her to court because she brought stone jugs of watered-down ale instead of quarts with seals guaranteeing quality. Sometimes you would call out for Cicely Hacket."

"Yes, she is the landlady's maiden daughter," Christopher Sly said.

The third servant said, "Why, sir, you know no such tavern and no such maiden daughter. You also do not know these men whom you have referred to: Stephen Sly and John Naps of Greet, a village near Stratford-upon-Avon. You also do not know Peter Turph and Henry Pimpernell and twenty more such names and men as these who have never existed and whom no one has ever seen."

"May God be thanked for my good improvement!" Christopher Sly said.

To that, everyone present said, "Amen."

"Thank you," Christopher Sly said. "You will be rewarded for your good wishes."

Dressed in women's clothing, Bartholomew, the Lord's page, entered the bedchamber, along with some servants.

"How fares my noble Lord?" Bartholomew asked.

"I fare well because here is lots of hospitable entertainment," Christopher Sly replied.

He added, "Where is my wife?"

"Here I am, my noble Lord," Bartholomew replied. "What do you want?"

"Are you my wife and will not call me husband?" Christopher Sly said. "My men should call me 'Lord.' I am your goodman: your husband."

"You are my husband and my Lord, my Lord and my husband," Bartholomew said. "I am your wife in all obedience. I have promised to love, honor, and obey you."

"I well know it," Christopher Sly replied.

He asked the others present, "What must I call her?"

The Lord replied, "Madam."

"Alice Madam, or Joan Madam?" Christopher Sly asked.

"Just 'Madam,' and nothing else," the Lord said. "That is the way that Lords call their wives."

"Madam Wife, they say that I have dreamed and slept some fifteen years or more," Christopher Sly said.

"That is true, and the time seems like thirty years to me," Bartholomew said. "All those years I have been banished from your bed."

"That is a very long time," Christopher Sly said.

He added, "Servants, leave me and her alone."

He then said to Bartholomew, "Madam, undress and come to bed now."

Thinking quickly, Bartholomew said, "Three times noble Lord, let me beg of you to excuse me from fulfilling your request until a night or two have passed, or, if you will not, to wait until the Sun sets. Your physicians have strictly ordered me to stay out of your bed for a while because you are still at risk of becoming ill again. I hope that you accept this reason for my staying out of your bed at this time. I hope that you will let this reason stand."

"This reason is not the only thing standing," Christopher Sly, glancing at a bump in the bedding immediately over his crotch. "It will be difficult for me to wait a day or two or even until the Sun sets. However, I would hate to fall ill and vanish into my dreams again. I will therefore wait to bed you despite what my flesh and the blood in it urge me to do."

A messenger entered the bedchamber and said, "Your honor's actors, hearing about your improvement, have come to perform a pleasant comedy because your doctors believe it will be good for you. Your doctors believe that you are much too sad and that your sadness has slowed your blood. They also believe that melancholy leads to madness. Therefore, they thought it good that you watch a play that will fill your mind with mirth and merriment. Laughter prevents a thousand harms and lengthens life."

"I will watch it; let the actors perform it," Christopher Sly said. "But what is a comondy? Is it a Christmas game or dance, or is it a tumbling-trick and acrobatics?"

Bartholomew thought, *He is unfamiliar with the word "comedy."*

Bartholomew said, "No, my good Lord; a comedy is more pleasing stuff."

"What stuff — household stuff?" Christopher Sly said. "Like a husband stuffing a wife with semen?"

"It is a kind of history," Bartholomew said.

"Well, we will see it," Christopher Sly said. "Come, Madam Wife, sit by my side and let the world slip by. Right now is the youngest that we will be for the rest of our lives."

CHAPTER 1
— 1.1 —

Lucentio and Tranio, his servant, had just arrived in Padua, Italy. They were conversing in a public street.

Lucentio said, "Tranio, I have always wanted to see beautiful Padua, nursery of learning and home of a famous university founded in 1228. I have now arrived in Padua while on my way to fruitful Lombardy, which is the pleasant garden of great Italy. With my father's love and permission, I have come here with his good will and your good company. My trusty servant, you have shown yourself to be good in every way. Here let us rest and perhaps begin a course of learning and ingenious studies.

"I was born in Pisa, which is renowned for grave and serious citizens, and my father, a merchant of great business throughout the world, was born there before me. My father is Vincentio, whose great and wealthy family is the Bentivolii. I, Vincentio's son, was brought up in Florence. It is only right that I should fulfill the hopes conceived of me, and add virtuous deeds of my own to my father's wealth and his own virtuous deeds.

"Therefore, Tranio, here I will study ethics and virtue and that part of philosophy that details how to achieve happiness by being virtuous — yes, I will study Aristotelian ethics. Aristotle taught that the way to become happy is through living a virtuous life.

"Tell me what you think. I have left Pisa and have come to Padua. I feel overwhelmed, like a man who leaves a shallow puddle and plunges into deep water and seeks to completely quench his thirst."

"*Mi perdonato* — pardon me — my gentle master," Tranio replied. "I am of the same mind as yourself; I think the same way that you think and feel the same way that you feel. I am glad that you thus continue your resolve to suck the sweets of sweet philosophy through its study.

"However, good master, while we do admire this virtue and this moral discipline, let us please not become Stoics or stocks. Stoics are philosophers who endure everything, and stocks are unfeeling blocks of wood that appreciate nothing. Let us take a middle path and appreciate the pleasures we have while enduring the pains we must. Let us not devote ourselves so completely to Aristotle's disciplines that we neglect to read Ovid, a poet of love and seduction. Let us not make Ovid an outcast in our lives.

"This is what I advise: Engage in formal argument and logic with the friends that you have and practice rhetoric — the art of communication — in your common conversation. Allow music and poetry to quicken and entertain your senses and your spirits. Study mathematics and metaphysics for only as long as you are interested in them. No profit can be acquired where no pleasure is taken: You will not learn unless you take pleasure in the learning. In brief, sir, study what you most enjoy."

"Many thanks, Tranio, you advise me well," Lucentio said.

He added, "If Biondello, my other servant, had come ashore, we could at once get started and find a lodging fit to entertain the friends we will make here in Padua."

He noticed some people coming out into the street and said, "But wait. Who are these people?"

"I'm guessing that they are here to welcome us," Tranio said. He knew that was not true.

Several people arrived, including Baptista and his two daughters, Katherina and Bianca. Katherina was the older of the two young and pretty daughters. Also present were Gremio and Hortensio, both of whom were courting Bianca. Gremio was an old man. From a short distance away, Lucentio and Tranio watched them.

Baptista said to Gremio and Hortensio, "Gentlemen, beg me no more. You know that I have made up my mind. I will not allow Bianca, my younger daughter, to marry until Katherina has married. I know you well and respect you well. If either of you wishes to court Katherina, you have my permission to do so."

Gremio thought to himself, *Court Katherina? Cart her, more likely. Prostitutes and shrews are driven around in carts in public and humiliated. Of course, Katherina is not a prostitute — she is a shrew, an ill-mannered, disobedient, and rude woman. She is too rough for me.*

Gremio asked, "Hortensio, will you take a wife? Why not marry Katherina?"

Katherina said to her father, "Sir, are you trying to make a whore of me amongst these mates? Am I to be given to anyone who asks for me?"

Hortensio said, "Mates, young maiden! What do you mean by that? You will get no mate — no husband — until you are of a gentler and milder character."

"Sir, you shall never need to fear marrying me," Katherina said. "Indeed, marriage is not even halfway to my heart — I have no interest in marriage. But even if I did, I would prefer to hit you over your silly head with a three-legged stool and paint your face red with blood and treat you like a fool rather than marry you."

Hortensio replied, "From all such devils may the good Lord deliver us!"

"And may the good Lord deliver me from all such devils!" Gremio said.

Tranio said to Lucentio, "Master, here is some good entertainment. That wench is either stark raving mad or wonderfully ill mannered."

"But in the other young woman, I see a maiden's mild behavior and modesty," Lucentio said, adding, "Now be quiet, Tranio."

"Well said, master," Tranio said. "I will be quiet as you gaze your fill at that modest young maiden."

"Gentlemen, I hope that I may soon make good on what I have said — I hope to soon find a husband for Katherina," Baptista said.

He added, "Good Bianca, go inside now. We don't need you to be outside so that men can see you and fall in love with you and want to marry you. At least not until your sister is married. And don't be unhappy that you have to wait to get married until after your older sister is married. I will still love you, my girl."

Katherina said, "Bianca is her father's pet. She can make herself cry whenever she wants — she puts her finger in her eye."

Bianca replied, "Sister, be content although I am discontent."

She added to her father, "Sir, I will humbly obey you. My books and musical instruments shall be my company. I will read my books and practice my music in solitude."

"Tranio, when she speaks it is as if we are hearing the voice of Minerva, goddess of wisdom," Lucentio said.

"Signior Baptista, will you be so unnatural a father?" Hortensio asked. "I am sorry that our good will has caused grief for Bianca."

"Why will you cage Bianca up, Signior Baptista, because of this fiend of hell, her older sister?" Gremio asked. "Why make Bianca bear the punishment of Katherina's sharp tongue?"

"Gentlemen, I have made my decision," Baptista said. "You will have to be content with it. I will not change my mind."

Baptista thought, *Women should be married. If I will not allow Bianca to marry until after Katherina is married, perhaps Bianca's suitors will help me to find a husband for Katherina.*

He added, "Go inside the house, Bianca."

She obeyed.

Baptista said to Gremio and Hortensio, "Because I know that Bianca takes much delight in listening to music, playing musical instruments, and reading poetry, I plan to hire tutors to stay in my house and teach her. If you, Hortensio, or you, Signior Gremio, know any such tutors capable of teaching my young daughter, send them to me. I will pay intelligent tutors well; I am willing to spend liberally to raise and educate my children well. And so to you I say farewell."

He said to his older daughter, "Katherina, you may stay outside for now because I have more to say to Bianca."

Baptista went inside his house.

Katherina said, "I trust I may go inside the house, too — why shouldn't I? What, shall I be appointed hours for when I can see my own father? Does he think that I am so stupid that I don't know what is valuable, that I don't know what to take and what to leave behind?"

She went inside the house.

Gremio, the old man who was hoping to marry Bianca, said about Katherina, "You may go to the devil's dam — the devil's mother is even worse than the devil! The devil's mother is the archetypal shrew! Your character is such that no one will stop you from leaving!"

To Hortensio, Gremio said, "Our love of women is not so important that we cannot wait patiently and do without for a while. Neither of us has gotten Bianca for a wife, and our failure is as if we have gotten a badly baked cake — our cake is mostly dough. Farewell. Yet, because of the love I bear my sweet Bianca, if I can by any means find a fit man who can teach her that wherein she delights, I will recommend him to her father."

"So will I, Signior Gremio," Hortensio replied, "but listen to me, please. Though the nature of our competition for Bianca's hand in marriage has never allowed us to really talk to each other, we should realize that now we ought to work together so that we may yet again have access to our fair mistress and be happy rivals in Bianca's love. If we work together to effect one thing specially, we can return to wooing Bianca."

"What thing is that, I ask?"

"Sir, to get a husband for her sister, Katherina."

"A husband! You must mean a devil!"

"I say, a husband."

"And I say, a devil. Do you think, Hortensio, that although Katherina's father is very rich, any man would be so great a fool as to be married to a hellion?"

"Tush, Gremio, although it is beyond your patience and mine to endure her loud and startling cries, why, man, there are good fellows in the world, if a man could find them, who would take her with all her faults, and with quite a lot of money."

"I don't know about that, but I do know that I would just as soon take her dowry with the condition that I be publicly whipped at the center of town every morning as I would with the condition that I endure her shrewishness."

"As you say, there is little choice when it comes to choosing between rotten apples," Hortensio said. "But, this obstacle to a possible future happy married life with Bianca should make us temporary friends and allies, and so we ought to work together to help Baptista's elder daughter, Katherina, to find a husband so that we can set his younger daughter, Bianca, free to find a husband. After we accomplish that, we can go back to being rivals and competitors.

"Sweet Bianca! May the winner's prize make him happy! He who runs fastest gets the ring — the prize of a wedding ring. What do you say, Signior Gremio?"

"I am agreed, and I would give Katherina's suitor the best horse in Padua to begin his wooing if he would thoroughly woo her, wed her and bed her, and rid the house of her! Let's go."

Gremio and Hortensio exited.

Tranio looked at Lucentio and realized that Lucentio was in love. He asked, "Is it possible that you can have fallen in love so quickly?"

"Tranio, until it happened to me, I never thought it was possible or likely, but while I idly stood and watched this scene, I found the effect of the flower named love-in-idleness, which causes people to fall in love. And now I honestly do confess to you, who are to me as trustworthy and as dear as Anna was to her sister, Dido, the Queen of Carthage, that I burn and I long for this young maiden named Bianca. I will perish, Tranio, if I do not win this young modest girl as my wife. Give me good advice, Tranio, for I know that you can. Help me, Tranio, for I know that you will."

"Master, it is not the right time to scold you. Scolding you will not drive love from your heart. If love has touched you, nothing remains but this: '*Redime te captum quam queas minimo*' — 'Ransom yourself from captivity as cheaply as you can.'"

"Many thanks, lad," Lucentio said. "Continue. What you have said pleases me. The rest of what you have to say will also please me because you give me good advice."

"Master, you looked so long and so longingly on the maiden that I am afraid that you did not notice what is the most important thing facing you."

"I saw sweet beauty in her face," Lucentio said. "Such beauty Europa, the daughter of Agenor, had. Jupiter fell in love with her, assumed the form of a bull, and carried her away to Crete. Jupiter knelt before her and kissed her hand. Europe was named after her."

"Didn't you notice anything else?" Tranio asked. "Didn't you notice how her older sister, Katherina, began to scold and raise up such a storm that mortal ears could hardly endure the din?"

"Tranio, I saw Bianca's coral lips move — with her breath she perfumed the air. Everything I saw in her was sacred and sweet."

Tranio said to himself, "It is time for me to wake him from his trance."

To Lucentio, he said, "Please, wake up, sir. If you love the maiden, take thought and use your wits to win her. This is how it stands: Her older sister is so curst and ill tempered that until the father rids his hands of her, your loved one must live and stay at home. Her father has tightly caged her up so that no suitors can woo her."

"Ah, Tranio, what a cruel father he is! But let us remember that he is taking some care to get knowledgeable schoolmasters to tutor her."

"I know that, sir, and I have a plan."

"So do I," Lucentio said.

"I am guessing that we have both come up with the same plan."

"Tell me your plan first," Lucentio said.

"You will pretend to be a tutor and undertake to teach the maiden. Is that your plan, too?"

"It is. Can it be done?"

"It is not possible," Tranio said, "for who shall play your part, and pretend to be you, Vincentio's son, in Padua here. Who will stay in your house and study your books, welcome your friends, and visit your countrymen and entertain them?"

"*Basta* — enough. Don't worry. I know what to do. We have not yet been seen by anyone, and so no one knows our faces. No one knows who is the master and who is the servant. Therefore, Tranio, you shall pretend to be me. You will live in my dwelling and live my lifestyle and hire servants to wait on you just as if you were me. I will pretend to be someone else — some Florentine, or some Neapolitan, or a lower-class man of Pisa. That is our plan. Tranio, take off your servant's dark-colored hat and cloak and instead put on my brightly colored hat and cloak."

They exchanged hats and cloaks.

"When Biondello comes, he will pretend to be your servant and wait on you. I will talk to him first so that he will hold his tongue and keep our secret."

"It is a good idea to talk to Biondello and advise him what to do," Tranio said. "Sir, I am required to be obedient, for so your father ordered me to be at our parting — he said, 'Do your best to serve my son' — although I do not think that he had this in mind. Because of his order and because this is what you want me to do, I am happy to pretend to be Lucentio because I love and respect Lucentio."

"Tranio, be of good service to me because I am in love. I will pretend to be a tutor — a servant — in order to win Bianca as my wife — the young woman with whom at first sight I have fallen in love."

Lucentio looked up and said, "Here comes the rogue — my servant Biondello — now."

Biondello walked up to them.

"What have you been up to?" Lucentio asked him.

"What have I been up to!" Biondello said. "What have you two been up to? Master, has my fellow Tranio stolen your clothes? Or have you stolen his? Or have each of you stolen the other's clothes? Just what is going on?"

"Listen, this is no time to jest," Lucentio said. "Behave soberly because the situation demands it."

He then began to lie to convince Biondello to be quiet about the exchange of identities: "Your fellow Tranio here, to save my life, has put on my apparel and is pretending to be me. I have put on his apparel and am pretending to be him in order to save my life. After I came ashore, I quarreled with and killed a man and I am afraid that I was seen. Pretend to be Tranio's servant — that's an order. I need you to do that while I run away from here to save my life. Do you understand?"

"Do I understand? Of course!" Biondello said, but he thought, *Do I understand? Of course not!*

"And be sure not to call Tranio by his real name. Tranio is now Lucentio."

"Good for him," Biondello said. "I wish that I could say the same thing about me."

Tranio said, "I would grant your wish if granting it meant that Lucentio indeed would win Baptista's younger daughter as his wife. But my promotion is not for my sake but for Lucentio's. Please be careful to address me as Lucentio in public and whenever other people are around. When we are alone, why, then I am Tranio. But when we are not alone, I am Lucentio, your master."

"Tranio, let's go," Lucentio said. "One thing more needs to be done, and you will have to do it. You will have to be one of the suitors wooing Bianca. If you ask me why, I will not tell you, except to say that I have very good reasons for why you should do it."

The actors exited, and the first servant said to Christopher Sly, "My Lord, you nod and are ready to fall asleep. You are not watching the play."

"Yes, I am," Christopher Sly said. "It is a good play, surely. Is there any more of it?"

Bartholomew said, "My Lord, it has barely begun."

"It is a very excellent piece of work, Madam Lady," Christopher Sly said, but he thought, *I wish the play were over!*

Petruchio and his servant Grumio stood on a street in front of Hortensio's house in Padua.

Petruchio said, "Verona, for a while I have taken my leave of you so that I could travel to see my friends in Padua. Of all my friends, my best beloved and approved friend is Hortensio, and I think that this is his house. Grumio, knock here, I say."

"Knock, sir! Whom should I knock? Has a man rebused your worship?"

Petruchio thought, *Rebused? He means, abused and rebuked. Grumio plays games with me and deliberately pretends to misinterpret what I order him to do. I have never been able to tame him and make him stop his misbehavior.*

"Knock here, and knock hard. Pound here, and pound hard."

"Pound you, sir! Who do you think I am! Why should I pound on you?"

"Knock here before this door. Knock hard, or I will knock your head."

"My master has grown quarrelsome," Grumio said. "If I follow your orders and knock hard on you before this door, I doubt very much that you will be pleased. I might hit you first, but you will hit me harder."

"You won't obey my orders!" Petruchio said. "If you won't knock, I will ring — I will either ring the bell or wring your ears. Since it is a servant's duty to ring the bell, I know what a master should do — I will make you sing *sol-fa* in pain."

He grabbed Grumio's ears and wrung — twisted — them.

Grumio fell to the ground and shouted, "Help! My master is insane!"

"Now knock when I tell you to knock!"

Hortensio came to the door of his house and said, "What's going on? What's the matter? My old friend Grumio! And my good friend Petruchio! How is everyone in Verona?"

"Signior Hortensio, have you come to break up the fight?" Petruchio asked, "*Con tutto il cuore, ben trovato* — with all my heart I am glad to see you."

Hortensio said, "Get up, Grumio, get up. We will settle this argument."

He said to Petruchio, "*Alla nostra casa ben venuto, molto honorato signor mio Petruchio* — welcome to our house, much honored Petruchio."

To Grumio, Hortensio said, "Get up. We will settle this quarrel."

"It does not matter what he alleged to you in Latin," Grumio replied.

There he goes again, Petruchio thought. *He is Italian, and he knows that we are speaking Italian, not Latin. He willfully misunderstands me.*

Grumio continued, "I now have a lawful reason to leave his service. Why, he ordered me to knock him and to pound on him! Is it fitting for a servant to obey such orders! He must be drunk or a card short of a full deck! Maybe I should have obeyed his orders. Maybe things would have worked out better for me."

"He is a foolish villain!" Petruchio said. "Good Hortensio, I ordered the rascal to knock on your door and for the life of me I could not get him to do it."

"Knock on the door!" Grumio said. "Hardly! You spoke to me and clearly said, 'Knock here, and knock hard. Pound here, and pound hard.' I didn't know that you were talking about the door! What else was I to think other than you were ordering me to hit you and to pound on you? And you tell me now that you were ordering me to knock on the door?"

"Either get out of here, or shut up," Petruchio said to Grumio. "I am warning you."

"Petruchio, have patience," Hortensio said. "Grumio will behave now. Why, this is a bad business between you and him. Grumio is your old, trusty, amusing servant. And tell me now, sweet friend, what happy wind blows you here to Padua from old Verona?"

"It is such a wind as scatters young men throughout the world to seek their fortunes farther than at home where little experience can be found," Petruchio said. "But in a few words, Signior Hortensio, this is how it stands with me: Antonio, my father, has died, and I have thrust myself into this maze of a world to — with any luck — happily to wive and thrive as best I may. I have money in my wallet and property at home, and so I have come abroad to see the world and to seek a wife."

"Petruchio, should I speak frankly to you and tell you where to find a woman who would make a shrewish and ill-tempered and sharp-tongued wife? I am afraid that you would thank me but little for my information, yet I promise you she shall be rich — very rich. However, you are too good a friend of mine for me to wish that you would marry her."

"Signior Hortensio, between two such friends as we are, a few words are enough for us to understand each other," Petruchio said. "Therefore, if you know a woman who is rich enough to be Petruchio's wife — and I want to marry a rich woman — then tell me about her.

"I do not care if she is as foul as was the wife of Florentius, a knight who quested to find the answer to the question 'What do all women most desire?' An ugly hag gave him the right answer — 'to be the ruler of a man's love' — but he had to marry her. In that case, all worked out because on their wedding night, the ugly hag turned into a beautiful young woman, She, the daughter of the King of Sicily, had been enchanted.

"I also do not care if she is as old as the Sibyl who was granted a wish by Apollo, god of light and music. She reached down and grabbed as much sand as she could and then asked to live as many years as she held grains of sand in her hand. In this case, things did not work out. She forgot to ask for eternal youth, and so she grows older and older and older and when she is asked what she wants, she replies that she wants to die.

"I also do not care if she is shrewish as — or worse than — Xanthippe, the wife of Socrates. She was so shrewish that Socrates turned to philosophy to acquire the patience to cope with her.

"This shrew whom you are talking about does not frighten or worry me or lessen my desire to marry a rich wife, and she would not even if she were as rough and violent as the swelling Adriatic seas. I come to wive it wealthily in Padua; and if I wive it wealthily in Padua, then I will wive it happily in Padua.

"I do not care if she is ugly, old, and ill tempered. I do care that she is rich — if I am to marry her, she must bring money to me."

Petruchio clearly stated that what he looked for in a wife was the money that she would bring him. He also implied that money was all he looked for in a wife. However, his future actions would show that he wanted much more than just the money that a wife with a very rich father could bring him.

Grumio said, "My master speaks frankly and clearly. If you give him enough gold, he will be happy to marry a puppet or a small figurine or an old hag with not even a single tooth in her head even if she has as many diseases as fifty-two horses. Why, he will marry anything and see nothing amiss provided that he receives money from the marriage."

"Petruchio, since I have told you so much already, even though I was joking, I will continue to give you information about the shrew and her father," Hortensio said. "I can, Petruchio, help you to get a wife who has much wealth, who is young and beautiful, and who was brought up as best becomes a gentlewoman. Her only fault, and it is a grievous fault, is that she is intolerably curst and ill tempered and shrewish and perverse, so beyond all measure and to such an extreme that, were my financial situation far worse than it is, I would not wed her even if I were to get a gold mine in recompense."

"Hortensio, peace!" Petruchio said. "You don't know the effect that gold has on me. Tell me her father's name and it will be all I need; for I will board her as though I were a pirate attacking a merchant ship — even though she chide and grumble as loud as thunder when the clouds in autumn crack with lightning."

"Her father is Baptista Minola. He is an affable and courteous gentleman. Her name is Katherina Minola. She is famous in Padua for her sharp and scolding tongue."

"I know her father, though I do not know her. Her father knew my late father well. I will not sleep, Hortensio, until I see her. So therefore let me be thus so rude to you as to leave you so quickly after we have met — unless you will accompany me as I visit her father and her."

"Please, sir," Grumio said, "let him go while the mood lasts. I swear that if she knew Petruchio as well as I do, she would think that scolding him would have little effect upon him. She may perhaps call him 'knave' half a score times or so, but that's nothing to him. Why, once he begins to reply to her, he will scold her with his own rope-tricks."

Petruchio thought, *Grumio means rhetoric or perhaps tricks that would best be punished by hanging — or perhaps both.*

Grumio continued, "I'll tell you what, sir, if she withstands him even a little bit, he will throw an insulting figure of speech in her face and so disfigure her with it that she shall have no more eyes to see with than a cat that has been fighting with another cat that has scratched out its eyes."

"Wait a moment, Petruchio," Hortensio said. "I will go with you. For in Baptista's keep — his inner sanctum — he keeps my treasure. There he hides away his younger daughter, beautiful Bianca, the jewel of my life. He is keeping her away from me and from all her other suitors — my rivals for her love. Baptista wants Katherina to be married. Knowing how difficult — or perhaps impossible — it is for such a marriage to take place because of her shrewish defects that I have told you about, Baptista has decreed that no suitor shall have access to Bianca until Katherina the curst — the ill tempered — has gotten a husband. Baptista is clever: He believes that by not allowing Bianca to be married until Katherina is married, Bianca's suitors will help him find a husband for Katherina."

Grumio declared, "Katherina the curst! Katherina the ill tempered! Those are the worst titles for a maiden who is the worst!"

"Petruchio, my friend, I want you to do me a favor," Hortensio said. "I will disguise myself with a beard and sober academic clothing so that I look like a fully qualified tutor, and you, Petruchio, will introduce me to old Baptista and recommend that I become a music tutor to Bianca. With this trick, I will have the opportunity to see her. Unsuspected by Baptista, I can be alone with Bianca and woo her."

"Here's no knavery!" Grumio said sarcastically. "Look at how the young folks lay their heads together to find a way to fool the old folks!"

Gremio and Lucentio, who was disguised as a tutor, appeared on the street in front of Hortensio's house.

Grumio said to Hortensio, "Look! Who are those people?"

"Be quiet, Grumio," Hortensio replied. "The older man is my rival for the love of Bianca."

He added, "Petruchio, let us stand here, off to the side, for a while and spy on them."

Grumio said sarcastically about Gremio, an old man, "He is a fine young man and an amorous and romantic young man!"

Gremio said to the disguised Lucentio, "Very well. I have read over this list of books for when you tutor Bianca. Buy them unbound and have them very beautifully bound. Make sure that they are all books about love — do not give her any other kind of lessons because I want her to think about love and marriage. You understand me. Signior Baptista will pay you to tutor Bianca; I will give you additional money to represent my interests. Take the paper that you will use in the lessons and let me have it very well perfumed because Bianca is sweeter than perfume itself. What will you read to her?"

"Whatever I read to her, I will plead your love for her as well and strongly as if you, my patron, were standing in front of her. I may even be able to plead your case better than you yourself could — unless you were a scholar, sir."

"What a wonderful thing learning is!" Gremio said. "Scholars are so proficient with words that they must be very wise."

"What a wonderful ass is this stupid woodcock!" Grumio said. "Woodcocks are so easily caught in traps that they must be very stupid."

"Be quiet!" Petruchio said to Grumio.

"Grumio, be quiet," Hortensio said.

He then said, "God bless you, Signior Gremio."

"We are well met, Signior Hortensio," Gremio replied. "Do you know where I am going? To visit Baptista Minola. I promised to inquire carefully about a tutor for the beautiful Bianca, and by good fortune I have found this young man, who is just the tutor she needs. He is learned and has good manners, and he is well read in poetry and other books — all of them good ones, I promise you."

"That is good," Hortensio replied. "I myself have met a gentleman who has promised to help me to find an additional tutor for Bianca: a fine musician. Therefore, I will also be able to serve beautiful Bianca, who is so beloved by me."

"She is so beloved by me," Gremio said. "My deeds will prove that."

"So will his moneybags," Grumio said.

"Gremio, this is not the time to express our love for Bianca," Hortensio said. "Listen to me, and if you are polite, I will tell you news that is equally good for both of us. Here is a gentleman whom I met by chance. If you and I can come to a financial agreement that is acceptable to him, he will woo curst Katherina — and marry her, if her dowry pleases him."

"If he actually does what he says he will do, it is good," Gremio said. "Hortensio, have you told him all her faults?"

Petruchio said, "I know she is an irksome and brawling scold. If that be all, sirs, I hear no harm that can stop me from wooing and marrying her."

"Are you sure?" Gremio asked. "Where are you from?"

"I was born in Verona, and I am old Antonio's son," Petruchio said. "My father is dead, and I inherited his fortune, and I hope to live a good and long life."

"Sir, such a life, with such a wife, is unlikely!" Gremio said. "But if you have a stomach for it, and you want to woo and marry Katherina, then go to it, by God! You shall have my help in so doing. But do you really intend to woo this wildcat?"

"Do I really intend to continue to breathe and to live?" Petruchio replied.

"Will he woo her?" Grumio said. "Yes, or I'll hang her. Why should she escape bad fortune? I am not sure which — Petruchio or the hanging — is the frying pan and which is the fire."

"Why have I come here but for the purpose of wooing and marrying her?" Petruchio said. "Do you think that a little din and racket can hurt my ears? Have I not in my time heard lions roar? Have I not heard the sea — puffed up with winds — rage like an angry boar coated with sweat? Have I not heard great cannon in the battlefield, and Heaven's artillery thunder in the skies? Have I not in a pitched battle heard loud calls to arms, neighing steeds, and the noise of trumpets? And you want me to be afraid of a woman's tongue, that gives not half so great a blow to the ears as will a chestnut popping in a farmer's fire? You would be better off trying to frighten boys with boogiemen."

Actually, Petruchio was a young man who was seeing the world for the first time. He had made up this exciting past history.

"Petruchio fears no shrews and no boogiemen," Grumio said.

"Hortensio, listen to me," Gremio said. "This gentleman of yours — Petruchio — is fortunately arrived, I think, for his own good and ours."

"I promised we would pay for his costs in wooing Katherina," Hortensio said.

"And so we will, provided that he wins and marries her," Gremio said.

"He will," Grumio said. "I would bet a good dinner on it and so be sure that I will be well fed."

Tranio, who was dressed in Lucentio's fine clothing, and Biondello, who was dressed in his usual servant's clothing, appeared on the street. They ignored the disguised Lucentio and pretended not to know him.

Tranio, Lucentio's servant who was disguised as Lucentio, said, "Gentlemen, God bless you. If I may be so bold, tell me, please, which is the readiest way to the house of Signior Baptista Minola?"

"The Signior Baptista Minola who has two daughters — is that the man you mean?" Biondello asked, making clear which man Tranio was asking about.

"Yes, that is the man, Biondello," Tranio said.

"Do you mean to see the daughter, sir?" Gremio asked.

"Perhaps I mean to see both him and her, sir," Tranio said, "but what business is it of yours?"

"I hope that you are not going to see the daughter who is the shrew," Petruchio said.

"I don't care for shrews," Tranio replied. "Biondello, let's go."

Quietly, Lucentio said to Tranio, "Your pretending to be me is off to a good start. Well done."

"Sir, a word before you go," Hortensio said. "Are you a suitor to the maiden you talked about — the one who is not a shrew. Yes or no?"

"And if I am a suitor to her, sir, is that a problem?" Tranio replied.

"No," Gremio said, "if without more words you will leave here."

"Why, sir, I ask you, are not the streets here as free to be used by me as to be used by you?"

"The streets are for both of us, but Bianca is not," Gremio said.

"For what reason?" Tranio asked.

"For this reason, if you want to know — she is the chosen and choice love of Signior Gremio," Gremio said.

"She is the chosen and choice love of Signior Hortensio," Hortensio said.

"Just a moment," Tranio said. "If you are gentlemen, do this for me: Listen patiently to me. Baptista is a noble gentleman, to whom my father is not completely unknown. His daughter is beautiful, and she is entitled to many suitors, including me. This would be true even if she were more beautiful — or less beautiful — than she is. Fair Leda's daughter Helen, the most beautiful woman in the world, had a thousand wooers, and so fair Bianca may have one more suitor — and so she does. I, Lucentio, would woo her even if Paris, Prince of Troy, came here in hopes to woo her all alone and to make her Helen of Troy."

"Wow! This gentleman will out-talk us all," Gremio said.

"Sir, do not check him the way that you would a horse," Lucentio said. "Let him run unchecked. He will show himself to be a jade — a weak horse that will quickly tire and quit."

"Hortensio, what is going on here?" Petruchio said. "Why is everyone arguing?"

Hortensio ignored Petruchio and said to Tranio, "Let me ask you, have you ever seen Baptista's daughter?"

"No, sir," Tranio replied, "but I hear that he has two daughters. One daughter is as famous for her scolding tongue as the other is for beauteous modesty."

"Sir, I will woo the daughter with the scolding tongue," Petruchio said. "Do not attempt to woo her."

"Good idea," Gremio said. "Leave that labor to great Hercules. He is already known for his twelve labors — hereafter let him be known for a thirteenth labor."

"Sir, understand this," Petruchio said. "The younger daughter — the one whom you should woo — her father keeps away from all suitors. He will not allow her to be married to any man until her elder sister the shrew is first wed. Only then will the younger daughter be free to marry and not before."

Tranio replied, "If it is true, sir, that you are the man who will help all of Bianca's suitors, including me, to gain access to her after you break the ice and get married to the elder daughter and so set free the younger daughter, then whoever shall win and marry Bianca will not be so ill-bred as to be ungrateful to you. You will be rewarded."

"Sir, you speak well, and well do you understand what is in fact happening here," Hortensio said. "Since you confess that you are a suitor to Bianca, you must do as we do and gratify this gentleman, Petruchio, with money to pay the cost of wooing Katherina, the shrewish elder daughter. All of us will benefit if he marries her — once he marries Katherina, we can woo Bianca."

"Sir, I will pay my part of the expenses," Tranio said. "To seal our pact, let us get together this afternoon and drink toasts to Bianca's health. We will do what prosecuting lawyers and defense lawyers do — combat each other mightily in the arena but eat and drink as friends."

Both Grumio and Biondello said, "Excellent idea. Let's go."

Hortensio agreed: "Good idea, indeed. Let's do it. Petruchio, I will be your host and pay for your drinks."

CHAPTER 2

— 2.1 —

In a room in Baptista's house, Katherina was tormenting Bianca, whose hands Katherina had tied together.

Bianca pleaded, "Good sister, do not hurt me or your reputation by making a slave of me. That is something I hate and will not endure. But if you want, you can have my possessions. I am wearing jewelry. If you will untie my hands, I will take it all off myself and give it to you. You can even have my clothing — I will strip myself down to my petticoat. Or I will do whatever else you command me to do — I know my duty is to obey my elders."

"I order you to tell me which of your suitors you like the best," Katherina said. "Make sure that you do not lie to me."

"Believe me, sister, of all the men alive now I have never yet beheld a special face that I could fancy more than any other. I have no preference for any of my suitors."

Katherina was interested in marriage and suitors, but she had no suitors of her own.

She said to Bianca, "You are lying! Do you prefer Hortensio?"

"If you like him, sister, I swear here and now that I will plead to him to woo you ... if there is no other way for you to have him."

"Perhaps you fancy riches more than you do youth. You must want to marry Gremio so that he will buy you fine clothing."

"Is it because of him that you envy me so? No, you are joking. Now I see that you have been joking with me all this time. Please, sister Kate, untie my hands."

"If you think that I was just making a joke, then everything else was also a joke," Katherina said.

Baptista had heard the commotion, and now he came into the room in time to see Katherina hit Bianca.

"What are you doing, Dame Insolence!" Baptista said. "From where has come this bad behavior?"

He added, "Bianca, stand beside me. Poor girl! You are crying. Go and ply your needle and sew; have nothing to do with your sister."

As he untied Bianca's hands, he said to Katherina, "You should be ashamed, you good-for-nothing with a devilish spirit. Why are you hurting her who never did anything to hurt you? When has she ever said to you a cross word?"

"Her silence mocks me, and I will get revenge on her because of her silence," Katherina said.

She moved toward Bianca, but Baptista blocked her way and said, "You dare to try to hurt Bianca in my sight?"

He added, "Bianca, go to another room."

"Why won't you leave me alone?" Katherina said. "Now I see that Bianca is your treasure. She must have a husband, and as an unmarried older sister I must follow the custom of dancing barefoot on her wedding day — that is supposed to break my bad luck in being unmarried! And if I die unmarried, I am supposed to lead apes to Hell instead of leading children to Heaven. That is the fate of an old maid. Don't talk to me. I will go and sit and cry until I can find an occasion to wreak my revenge on my sister."

Katherina exited.

Baptista watched her go and then said, "Has any man ever been so beset by troubles as I am?"

Several people now entered the room. Gremio and Petruchio walked in. So did Lucentio, who was disguised as a tutor. So did Hortensio, who was disguised as a musician. So did Tranio, who was disguised as Lucentio. Bringing up the rear was Lucentio's servant Biondello, who was carrying books and the stringed musical instrument known as the lute.

"Good day, neighbor Baptista," Gremio said.

"Good day, neighbor Gremio," Baptista said, adding, "God bless you all, gentlemen!"

"And you, too, good sir!" Petruchio said. He added, "Don't you have a daughter named Katherina, who is beautiful and virtuous?"

The word "virtuous" bothered Baptista, who knew that his elder daughter was a shrew. He replied, "I have a daughter, sir, called Katherina."

Gremio wanted Petruchio to succeed in marrying Katherina. He advised him, "You are too blunt. First go slow and be sociable and then get down to business."

"You are mistaken, Signior Gremio," Petruchio said. "I know what I am doing."

He said to Baptista, "I am a gentleman of Verona, sir. Having heard of Katherina's beauty and her wit, her affability and bashful modesty, her wondrous qualities and mild behavior, I am now so bold as to make myself an eager guest in your house to make my eyes witnesses of that report which I so often have heard. To show my appreciation for your hospitality and to pay for my entrance into your house, I present you with a recommendation for a servant of mine."

He pointed to the disguised Hortensio and said, "This man here is knowledgeable in music and in mathematics. He is entirely capable of teaching your daughter those two sciences, of which I know that she is not ignorant. Accept my recommendation of him, or else you do me wrong: His name is Litio, and he was born in Mantua."

"You are welcome here, sir," Baptista said to Petruchio, "and Litio is also welcome here, for your sake. But as for my daughter Katherina, I know that she is not the girl you want, which is a pity for me."

"I see that you do not mean to part with her," Petruchio said, "or else you do not like my company."

"Please don't misunderstand me," Baptista said. "I am saying only what I believe is the truth. But where are you from? And what is your name?"

"Petruchio is my name; I am Antonio's son. He was a man well known throughout all Italy."

"I have heard much about him," Baptista said. "You are welcome here for his sake."

Gremio said, "With all respect for your story, Petruchio, let us, who are humble suitors for Bianca, speak, too. *Backare!* Back off a little! You are too pushy!"

"Oh, pardon me, Signior Gremio; I am eager to be doing what needs to be done."

He thought, *What needs to be done is my wooing of and marrying Katherina. Once I have married her and am sure of having a good wife, then she will need to be done and I will do her. I want a warm wife and a warm bed.*

"I doubt it not, sir," Gremio said, "but you will curse your wooing if you are too eager. Neighbor Petruchio, this recommendation of a tutor is a gift very grateful to Baptista — I am sure of it."

He added to Baptista, "To express the same kindness, I myself, who have been more in your debt than any other man, freely recommend to you this young scholar."

He pointed to the disguised Lucentio and said, "He has long studied at the renowned university in Rheims, France. He is as well educated in Greek, Latin, and other languages as the other tutor is well educated in music and mathematics. His name is Cambio; please accept his services."

"A thousand thanks, Signior Gremio," Baptista said.

He said to the disguised Lucentio, "Welcome, good Cambio."

To Tranio, who was pretending to be Lucentio, he said, "Gentle sir, I think that you have the bearing of a stranger in town. May I be so bold as to ask you why you have come here?"

"Pardon me, sir," Tranio said. "The boldness is my own. I am a stranger in this city, and I have come here to make myself a suitor to your daughter, the beautiful and virtuous Bianca. I know about your firm decision not to allow Bianca to be married until Katherina, her elder sister, is married. I request that once you know who my father is that you give me the same freedom as Bianca's other suitors to see her and to woo her. To help you educate your two daughters, I have brought you gifts. Here I give you a simple instrument — a lute — as well as this small packet of Greek and Latin books. If you accept them, then their worth is great. You will add to their value by accepting them."

Biondello handed Baptista the gifts.

"Lucentio is your name," Baptista said, looking at an inscription in one of the books. "Where are you from?"

"I am from Pisa, sir. My father is Vincentio."

"Vincentio of Pisa is a man of great power and influence. I have heard good reports of him, and you are very welcome here, sir."

Baptista said to the disguised Hortensio, "You take the lute," and then he said to the disguised Lucentio, "You take the set of books."

He then said to both of them, "You shall see your pupils now."

Baptista called for a servant and then said to him, "Take these gentlemen to my daughters and tell them both that these gentlemen are their tutors. Tell my daughters to be on their best behavior."

Lucentio, Hortensio, and the servant exited.

Baptista then said to those remaining, "We will go and walk a little in the garden, and then we will eat dinner. You are all very welcome here, and I hope that you will feel comfortable and at home here."

Petruchio was eager to start wooing Katherina, whom he still had not seen.

"Signior Baptista," he said, "my business requires haste. I cannot come every day here to woo Katherina. You knew my father well, and he has left me — his only heir — all his lands and possessions, which by good management I have increased rather than decreased their value. I am a man of property, and I am competent. I also get down to business quickly. Tell me, if I get your daughter Katherina to love me, what dowry will she bring to me when I marry her?"

"I have no sons. After my death, Katherina will get one half of my lands," Baptista said. "As soon as she is married, she will bring you 20,000 crowns."

"The dowry is acceptable," Petruchio said. "Now for the dower. As her husband, I must provide for my wife if I should die first. If Katherina should survive me, she will receive all of my lands and all of my leases. My widow — should my wife outlive me — will receive a large income. Therefore, let us have legal contracts drawn up between us, so that each of us is legally obligated to do what we have promised to do."

"We will do so," Baptista said, "once you have gotten something that is very special: Katherina's love. That is the most special thing of all — it is much more important than wealth, property, and income."

Baptista thought, *Katherina is special. I want her to be happy, and she will be happily married only if she marries a man whom she can respect. Bianca, on the other hand, will — I am sure — marry whatever man I want her to. She will be happy with that man. In her case, I can have her marry her wealthiest suitor. After all, wealth is in fact important, although it is not the most important thing.*

"I will get her love. I promise you that, father — and you will be my father," Petruchio said. "I am as fiercely determined as she is proud-minded. When and where two raging fires meet together, they consume the things that feed their fury. Although a small fire grows big with a little wind, extreme gusts of wind will blow out all the fire. That is the way that it will be with Katherina and me.

I will be the great gust of wind that blows out her fire. She may be shrewish, but I am rough and I do not woo like a boy."

Petruchio thought, *This metaphor, properly understood, states that both Katherina and I will change our behavior. Like the two fires, we will blow each other out. She will yield to me, and then I will yield to her. I will persuade her to change her behavior from a shrew to a wife who will love, honor, and obey me. "Persuade" is the right word; "force" is not the right word. The kind of change I want is the kind that cannot be forced, although a lot of persuasion is appropriate. To do that, I will assume a behavior that is different from my usual behavior, but I will cast off that behavior once I have the wife that she will promise before God — in the marriage ceremony — that she will be: a wife who loves, honors, and obeys her husband. And I will do what I will promise before God — in the marriage ceremony — that I will do: I will love and cherish my wife.*

Petruchio had impressed Baptista, who thought, *Petruchio may be exactly the right man to woo and marry Katherina. Make no mistake, Katherina needs to be tamed. Just a few minutes ago, she tied up and beat her sister. No one deserves to be so badly treated — especially a relative. I think that Katherina is intelligent. I would not be surprised if Katherina knows that she needs to be tamed. Neither I nor Katherina — I think — wants her to keep on acting the way she has been acting.*

Baptista said to Petruchio, "I hope that you woo Katherina well, and good luck to you! But be prepared for some unhappy words that she will call you."

"When it comes to harsh words, I am wearing tested steel armor," Petruchio said. "I can withstand harsh language the way that mountains withstand winds. Mountains do not shake no matter how hard the wind blows."

The disguised Hortensio now entered the room. The lute that Tranio had given to Baptista was now broken — and so was Hortensio's head.

"Hello, my friend," Baptista said. "Why do you look so pale?"

"I am pale from fear," Hortensio said. "You can be sure of that."

"Will my daughter Katherina become a good musician?" Baptista asked.

"I think she will sooner become a good soldier," Hortensio said. "Pistols and bullets may withstand her treatment, but never lutes."

"So you are saying that you cannot teach her to play the lute? You cannot break down the steps of playing a lute?"

"No, I cannot," Hortensio said, "because she has broken the lute on my head. All I did was to tell her that her hands were not placed correctly on the frets of the lute. She got angry and said, 'Do you think that I am fretting? I will show you that I am fuming!' With that word, she struck me on the head with the lute and both my head and the lute broke. There I stood amazed for a while with the lute around my neck like a wooden collar. She called me names — rascal fiddler and twangling Jack, and twenty more such vile terms. It was as if she had memorized the names just to be prepared to insult me with them."

"By God, Katherina is a spirited wench," Petruchio said. "She is full of life, and now I love her ten times more than ever I did. How I long to talk to her!"

Baptista said to Hortensio, "Come with me and do not be so discouraged. Go and tutor my younger daughter. She is eager to learn and thankful for good tutoring."

He added, "Signior Petruchio, will you go with us, or shall I send my daughter Kate to you?"

"Please send Kate to me," Petruchio said.

Everyone left except for Petruchio.

Alone, Petruchio planned his course of action in dealing with the shrew whom he wanted to marry: "I will wait for her here and woo her with some spirit when she comes. If she shouts at me, why then I'll tell her plainly that she sings as sweetly as a nightingale. If she frowns, I'll say she looks as cheerful as morning roses newly washed with dew. If she is mute and will not speak a word, then I will compliment her talkativeness and say that she is speaking with moving eloquence. If she orders me to leave, I will give her thanks as though she asked me to stay by her for a week. If she refuses to wed me, I will ask her to name the day when our engagement will be announced and when we will be married. I will treat her as if she were already the good woman I want her to be. I will give her a good image of herself."

He saw Katherina enter the room and said to himself, "Here she comes now. Petruchio, speak to her."

To Katherina, he said, "Good day, Kate, for that is your name, I hear."

"You are somewhat hard of hearing. People who talk about me call me Katherina."

"Truly, you lie," Petruchio said. "You are called plain Kate, and you are called pretty Kate and sometimes Kate the curst, but you are Kate, the prettiest

Kate in the Christian world. You are Kate of Kate Hall, and you are my super-dainty Kate. Dainty cakes are delicacies, and you are a delicacy. Therefore, Kate, listen to my comforting words. Hearing your mildness praised in every town, your virtues spoken of, and your beauty complimented, yet not to the degree you deserve, I am moved to woo you to be my wife."

"Moved, are you?" Katherina said. "Let whoever moved you here now remove you from here. The moment I saw you I knew that you were a moveable."

"Why, what's a moveable?" Petruchio asked.

"A wooden stool — something that is hard like your head."

"A stool has hard wood to be sat on, so come, Kate, and sit on me."

"Asses are made to bear, and so are you. Bear a load, you ass."

"Women are made to bear, and so are you. Women bear children, and in order to become pregnant, they bear the weight of a man in the missionary position."

"I have no intention of bearing your children or your weight. You are a jade, a horse without stamina, and I doubt that you have stamina in bed."

Petruchio thought, *I am not a rapist. I want to marry Kate, but I do not want to consummate the marriage with a meeting of bodies until after Kate and I have had a meeting of minds.*

"Not yet will I have you bear the burden of my weight," Petruchio said, "because you are young and light —"

"I am too light for such a country bumpkin as you to catch, and yet I am as heavy as my weight should be. I am not like a gold coin whose edge has been shaved and so is worth less than it ought to be."

"Be! Bee! Buzz! I hope that you can avoid the buzzing that would surround you if you became the subject of gossip," Petruchio said. "Light women are often the subject of gossip because it is easy to move them into a position for sexual intercourse."

Katherina said, "'Buzz' is what I would expect you to say — you are like a buzzard."

"You are like a slow-winged turtledove — the symbol of faithful love! Shall a buzzard take you?"

"If a buzzard should take me for a turtledove, the buzzard is mistaken."

"Come, come, you wasp; truly, you are too angry."

"If I am waspish, you had best beware my sting," Katherina said.

"My remedy is to pluck your sting out. That way, I need not fear it."

"That is a good remedy — if you, a fool, could find out where my sting is."

"Who does not know where a wasp keeps its sting? In its tail."

"No, the sting is in the tongue."

"Whose tongue?"

"Yours, if you talk of tales, and so I say farewell to you."

"What, with my tongue in your tail?" Petruchio said.

He said to Katherina, "Good Kate, I am a gentleman."

"I will see whether you are a gentleman," Katherina said, and she hit him.

Petruchio looked her in the eyes and said, seriously, "I swear that I will hit you, if you hit me again."

Katherina decided not to hit him again.

She said, "If you do, you will lose your arms. If you hit me, you are no gentleman, and if you are no gentleman, why then, you will have no coat of arms."

"Are you a herald, Kate? If you are, then put me in your heraldic book that lists gentlemen! Let me be on good terms with you."

"If you are a gentleman, then what is your crest? What heraldic device do you have? What is on your heraldic badge? Is it the feathers on a bird's head? Is it the crest of a cock? Is it a coxcomb? My guess is that it is a coxcomb — the hat worn by a court fool."

"If you, Kate, will be my hen, then I will be a combless cock. A cock without a comb is nonthreatening and non-aggressive, and a husband should not threaten his wife."

"You will never be a cock of mine — you have the crow of a craven, defeated fighting-cock."

"Come, Kate, come; you must not look so sour."

"I always look sour when I see a sour crabapple."

"No crabapple is here, and so therefore do not look sour."

"A crabapple is here!"

"Then show it to me."

"If I had a mirror, I would."

"Are you saying that my face looks crabby?"

"I am surprised that such a young and inexperienced person as yourself realized that," Katherina said.

"By Saint George, I am too young and too strong for you."

"Yet you are withered."

"It is with cares."

"I don't care."

"Kate, listen carefully. You will not escape me."

"I will irritate you, if I stay here. Let me go."

"You will not irritate me, Kate. I find you quite gentle. I was told that you are rough and withdrawn and sullen, but the people who told me that lied because you are pleasant, full of fun, very courteous, and slow in speech — you think before you speak. You are as sweet as springtime flowers. You are unable to frown, to glare, and to bite your lip, as angry women do. You do not take pleasure in arguments, but instead you entertain your wooers with gentle, quiet, and friendly conversation."

He added, "Why does all the world say that you, Kate, metaphorically limp? The world is filled with slanderers! Kate, you are like the hazel tree. You are straight and slender and as brown in hue as hazel nuts, and you are sweeter than the nuts' kernels. I know you. You do not limp."

"Go away, fool, and give commands to your servants."

"Did ever the beautiful Diana, goddess of chastity, so become a grove of trees as you, Kate, become this chamber with your princess-like gait? You be Diana, and let her be Kate. Then let Kate be chaste and Diana be playful and amorous!"

"Where did you study all this fancy speech?"

"It is extempore. I have made it up on the spur of the moment, using my mother-wit."

"It is good that you had a witty mother! Otherwise, her son would have been witless."

"Am I not wise?"

"You are barely wise enough to keep yourself warm in cold weather."

"I have every intention of marrying you, Kate, and of keeping myself warm in your bed. Therefore, let us set all this chitchat aside, and I will speak plainly. Your father has consented that you shall be my wife; we have agreed upon your dowry. Whether you are willing to marry or not, I will marry you. Kate, I am the husband who is just right for you. I swear by this light, by means of which I see your beauty — your beauty that makes me love you — you must be married to no man but me. Because, Kate, I am the man — the husband — who was born to tame you, Kate, and bring you from a wild Kate to a Kate who is a loving, honoring, and obedient Christian wife like other housewife Kates."

Seeing Baptista, Gremio, and Tranio coming toward them, Petruchio added, "Here comes your father. Do not deny me. I must and will have Katherina as my wife."

Baptista said, "Signior Petruchio, how are you and my daughter getting along?"

"How should we get along but well, sir? How but well? It is impossible that I should not get along well with your daughter."

"How are you, my daughter Katherina?" Baptista said. "You look in the dumps — miserable."

"Are you calling me your daughter? Ha! You are showing quite a tender fatherly regard for me when you wish me to wed this one-half lunatic, this madcap ruffian, this swearing Jack, this man who thinks to get his own way by bluffing with words!"

"Father," Petruchio said, "the truth is that you and everyone else in the world who have talked about Kate have misunderstood her. If she seems shrewish, it is only an act. Katherina is not obstinate; she is as gentle as a dove. She is not hot; she is as temperate as the morning. Griselda was a medieval wife who was patient and submissive no matter how her husband provoked her; Kate will prove herself to be a second Griselda. The Roman wife Lucrece vowed — and meant that vow — to be faithful to her husband; Kate will prove herself to be a second Lucrece. Kate and I get along so well that we have agreed to be married on Sunday."

"I will see you hanged on Sunday before I will marry you," Katherina said.

Gremio said, "Did you hear that, Petruchio? She said that she will see you hanged on Sunday before she will marry you."

Tranio said, "Do you call that getting along well with her? We can say goodbye to our hopes of marrying Bianca."

Petruchio replied, "Relax, gentlemen. I choose her for myself. I am the one who is marrying her. As long as she and I are pleased with each other, you have nothing to worry about. She and I have decided, in private, when we were alone, that she will still be ill tempered and shrewish when she is around other people, although she is not when she and I are alone. I tell you, it is incredible to believe how much she loves me: She is the kindest and most darling Kate! She hugged and plied me with kiss after kiss and made promise after promise to love me forever. In the time it takes to blink an eye, she made me fall in love with her. You are newcomers to love! It is amazing to see, when a man and a woman are left alone and fall in love, how tame a timid man can make the most ill-tempered shrew."

He added, "Give me your hand, Kate."

He took her hand; she did not resist.

He said, "I will go to Venice to buy clothing for our wedding. Prepare and provide the feast, father, and invite the guests. I will be sure my Katherina shall be finely dressed."

Everyone except Katherina looked at Baptista, who was puzzled. What was going on? Did his daughter want to marry this man or not? Baptista looked at Katherina, who was looking at Petruchio. She had a small smile on her face.

Baptista thought, *Petruchio may be just the husband my daughter Katherina needs — and wants. He may be just the man to tame her bad behavior and make her a good Christian wife. If my daughter does not want to marry him, she will let me know. Petruchio is leaving to go to Venice, and so she and I will be able to be alone.*

He said, "I do not know what to say, Petruchio, but let us shake hands. God send you joy, Petruchio! You and Katherina will be married on Sunday."

Katherina thought, *I am intrigued by Petruchio, but am I intrigued enough to marry him although we have just met and we have spent all our time together engaging in a verbal combat — a battle of wits? Hell, yes!*

Gremio and Tranio said, "Amen! We will be witnesses to the wedding."

"Father, and wife, and gentlemen, adieu," Petruchio said. I am going now to Venice; Sunday will come very soon. We will have rings and things and a fine array of clothing. And kiss me, Kate — we will be married on Sunday."

Petruchio kissed Katherina, who did not kiss him back.

Petruchio and Katherina exited in different directions.

Gremio said, "Have two people ever decided to wed each other so quickly?"

"Indeed, gentlemen," Baptista said, "this is a risky venture. I am like a businessman who is making a desperate gamble in hopes of thereby profiting."

"Your daughter Katherina is like a commodity that was not being used," Tranio said. "Now she will either bring you happiness by making a good and happy marriage, or she will metaphorically perish on the seas."

"The profit that I seek is a quiet and peaceful marriage for Katherina," Baptista said.

Not meaning it, Gremio said, "I have no doubt that Petruchio has gotten a quiet catch."

He added, "But now, Baptista, let's talk about your younger daughter, Bianca. Now is the day we long have looked for: the day that you will choose a husband for her. I am your neighbor, and I am the man who wooed her first."

Tranio, who was still disguised as Lucentio and was trying to get Bianca as a wife for Lucentio, made his own pitch: "And I am one who loves Bianca more than words can witness, or your thoughts can guess."

Gremio replied, "Youngster, you cannot love so dearly as I."

"Graybeard, your love is ice cold," Tranio said.

"And your love is too hot. Skipping boy, back off. It is age that nourishes."

"But in ladies' eyes it is youth that flourishes."

"Calm down, gentlemen," Baptista said. "I will settle this quarrel. I believe that Bianca will be happy with whomever of you two I chose for her to marry, and therefore it is deeds — action and legal deeds, not talk — that must win the prize. Whoever of you two can give my daughter the greatest dower shall be her husband. So, Signior Gremio, what dower can you assure me she will get? If you die before she does, with what can she support herself?"

Baptista thought, *Hortensio was another of Bianca's suitors, but he has not been around for a while. Perhaps he has lost interest.*

Gremio replied, "First, as you know, my house within this city is richly furnished with silver and gold dishes and utensils. Bianca will have basins and ewers to wash her dainty hands. My wall hangings are all of expensive purple tapestry. I have stuffed my crowns in ivory strongboxes. My bedspreads are made of tapestry from Arras, France; these I store in chests made of cypress wood. I own expensive clothing, bed curtains and hangings and canopies, fine linen, cushions made in Turkey that are embroidered with pearls, valances made in Venice and decorated with gold needlework, pewter and brass and all things that belong to house or housekeeping. At my farm I have a hundred milk cows, sixty fat oxen standing in my stalls, and all things necessary for their maintenance. I myself am advanced in years, I confess, and if I die tomorrow, all of this is hers, provided that while I live Bianca will be only mine."

"That word 'only' is well chosen," Tranio said. "You have only a few possessions in comparison to me. Baptista, listen to me. I am my father's heir and only son; I need not share my father's estate with brothers when he dies. If I may have your daughter as my wife, I will leave her houses three or four as good — within the walls of rich Pisa — as the one house that Signior Gremio has in Padua. In addition, she will receive two thousand ducats each year in income from my fruitful land. All of this shall she receive as her dower."

Gremio looked shocked at such wealth.

Tranio said to him, "Are you shocked, Signior Gremio?"

Gremio said, "Two thousand ducats of annual income from the land!"

He thought, *The value of all my land does not reach two thousand ducats!*

Gremio said, "Bianca shall have everything that I mentioned previously, plus an argosy — a large merchant ship — that now is anchored in the harbor at Marseilles."

Tranio said, "Gremio, it is well known that my father has no less than three great argosies. In addition, he has two galliases — ships that are larger than galleys, and that use both sails and oars. He also has twelve watertight galleys in good repair. I will give all of this to Bianca, and I will give twice as much as whatever you offer next."

Gremio replied, "That is not necessary. I have already offered all that I have, and I have no more possessions to offer."

He said to Baptista, "If you like me and my offer, Bianca shall have me and all that is mine."

Tranio interrupted, "Why, then the maiden is mine. Out of all the men in the world, I have won her. You, Baptista, firmly promised that Bianca would be the wife of the man who offered her the most. Gremio has been outbid."

Baptista replied, "I must confess that your offer is the best. Now, your father must make this offer a legal obligation. If he does so, Bianca will be your wife. But if your father does not make your offer a legal obligation, then — pardon me — if you should die before your father, then what would happen to her dower?"

"That is a small point," Tranio said. "My father is old. I am young. I will outlive him."

Gremio asked, "And may not young men die, as well as old?"

"Well, gentlemen, I have made up my mind," Baptista said. "On this coming Sunday you know that my daughter Katherina is to be married. On the Sunday following that, Bianca will become your bride, Lucentio, as long as your father takes on this legal obligation. If your father will not, then Bianca will become the bride of Signior Gremio. And so, I take my leave of you, and I thank you both."

"Adieu, good neighbor," Gremio said as Baptista left.

Alone with Tranio, whom he understood to be Lucentio, Gremio said, "I do not believe that Bianca will marry you because I do not believe that your father will make this legal obligation. You have gambled by promising so much as your dower, and you will lose your bet. Your father would be a fool to give you everything, and in his old age to set his feet under your table and be totally dependent on you. Your promised dower is ridiculous. Old Italian fathers are foxes, my boy, and they are not so kind as to give away everything they have and be penniless."

Gremio exited.

Tranio said, "May vengeance be wreaked on your crafty withered hide! You are right. I have promised more than I can deliver. I have bluffed with a card that is a ten-spot — a card of lesser value than a Jack! It is my intention to do my master Lucentio good. The only thing that can be done now is for the pretend Lucentio — me — to get a pretend father. I will have to find someone to pretend to be Lucentio's father, Vincentio. That will be a wonder. Fathers commonly do get — that is, beget — their children; but in this case of wooing, a child shall get a father, if my cunning helps me to succeed in this plan."

CHAPTER 3

— 3.1 —

Lucentio, Hortensio, and Bianca were in a room of Baptista's house. Lucentio and Hortensio were acting as Bianca's tutors. Lucentio had disguised himself as Cambio, a tutor of languages and philosophy; Hortensio had disguised himself as Litio, a teacher of music and mathematics. Lucentio and Hortensio had told Bianca who they really were, but Lucentio and Hortensio still thought that each other was a real tutor.

Lucentio said to Hortensio, "Fiddler, stop. You are too pushy, sir. Have you so soon forgotten the way that Bianca's sister, Katherina, treated you? She broke a lute on your head."

"That was Katherina, the shrew," Hortensio said, "and this is Bianca, the patroness of heavenly harmony. Therefore, give me leave to have the prerogative of teaching Bianca first. After we have spent an hour studying music, you — you wrangling pedant — shall have an hour to tutor her."

"You are a preposterous ass," Lucentio said. "You have not read enough to know the reason why music was created! Music was created to refresh the mind of man after his studies or his usual toil. Therefore, give me time to teach Bianca literature and philosophy, and afterward, while I rest, you can teach her harmony."

"Your remarks are offensive! I will not stand for them!"

Bianca interrupted, "Why, gentlemen, you both do me wrong. It is not your decision which of you should teach me first. It is my decision — I am the one who gets to choose. I am no scholar in the schools; I am not a student who can be whipped. I learn my lessons as and when it pleases me. Stop your arguing. All of us sit down. Litio, take your musical instrument and go over there and play it for a while. Cambio's lesson will be over before you have tuned your lute."

"You will leave his lesson when I am in tune?" Hortensio asked.

"That will be never," Lucentio said. "Go on and try to tune your instrument."

Bianca asked, "When did our last lesson end?"

"It ended here, madam," Lucentio said. "We were studying this:

"*Hic ibat Simois; hic est Sigeia tellus*;
"*Hic steterat Priami regia celsa senis.*"

These lines mean, "Here ran the Simois River; here was the Sigeian land; /
Here stood the lofty palace of old Priam."

The lines are from Ovid, *Heroides* I, *Penelope Ulixi* [Penelope to Ulysses],
lines 33-34, but some Latin words are misquoted.

Bianca requested, "Construe them."

Lucentio replied, speaking quietly so that Hortensio could not hear,

"*Hic ibat* means *As I told you before*.

"*Simois* means *I am Lucentio*.

"*Hic est* means *The son of Vincentio of Pisa*.

"*Sigeia tellus* means *Disguised thus to get your love*.

"*Hic steterat* means *And that Lucentio who comes a-wooing*.

"*Priami* means *Is my servant Tranio*.

"*Regia* means *Who is pretending to be me*.

"*Celsa senis* means *So that that we might trick the pantaloon — the ridiculous
old man — who is named Gremio*."

Hortensio said, "Madam, my instrument is in tune."

"Let's hear it," Bianca said.

Hortensio strummed the strings.

Bianca said, "The treble is out of tune."

"Spit in the hole, man," Lucentio said, "and tune it again. The spit will make
the peg tighter and keep the string in tune."

Hortensio returned to tuning the lute.

Bianca said to Lucentio, "Now let me see if I can construe it:

"*Hic ibat Simois* means *I do not know you*.

"*Hic est Sigeia tellus* means *I do not trust you*.

"*Hic steterat Priami* means *Be careful that my music tutor does not hear you*.

"*Regia* means *Do not presume too much*.

"*Celsa senis* means *Do not despair*."

Hortensio said, "Madam, it is now in tune."

Lucentio replied, "All but the bass."

Hortensio muttered, "The bass of the tune is in tune; it is that base knave
Cambio who is out of tune. How fiery and forward this pedant Cambio is! I

swear that he is courting Bianca, the woman I love. Little pedant! I will keep an eye on you!"

Bianca said to Lucentio, "In time I may believe you, yet now I mistrust you."

"Do not mistrust me," Lucentio said.

He said loudly so that Litio — the disguised Hortensio — could hear, "Aeacides is another name for Ajax. It identifies him as the grandson of Aeacus."

Lucentio was partially right. He was referring to the next line of the quotation from Ovid that they had been working on. However, "Aeacides" means "grandson of Aeacus" and Aeacus had more than one grandson. In fact, scholars translate the Aeacides of the line as Achilles, grandson of Aeacus. Homeric warriors Great Ajax and Teucer was also grandsons of Aeacus.

Bianca, who knew more Latin and more mythology than her tutor, said, "I must believe my master, or else, I promise you, I would argue with you about this point. But let us let it go."

She said loudly, "Now, Litio, it is your turn to tutor me. Good tutors, take it not unkindly, please, that I have been pleasant with you both and have not taken sides."

Hortensio said to Lucentio, whom he thought was Cambio, "You may go and walk, and leave us for a while. My lessons have no music for three singers or three musicians."

"Are you so formal, sir?" Lucentio replied. "Well, I must wait for my next turn to tutor."

He thought, *And I must watch this tutor Litio because, unless I am deceived, our fine musician is falling in love with Bianca.*

Hortensio said quietly to Bianca, "Madam, before you touch the instrument, you must learn the correct fingering. To do that, I must begin by teaching you the fundamentals of this art. To teach you the scales more quickly, pleasantly, pithily, and effectually than any other music tutors can do, I have written out the scales in my own way."

"Why, I learned my scales long ago," Bianca protested.

"Nevertheless, please read the scales as written by Hortensio."

Bianca read, "I am the scales, the beginning of all harmony,

"*A re* means *Hortensio pleads his passion.*

"*B mi* means *Bianca, take him for your husband.*

"*C fa ut* means *He loves you with all his heart.*

"*D sol re* means *He has one clef and two notes. He has two identities —
Hortensio and Litio — but only one is real.*

"*E la mi* means *Show pity to me, or I will die.*"

Bianca complained, "Do you call this musical scales? I do not like it. Old fashions please me best. I am not so fussy that I will change tried, tested, and true rules for odd inventions."

A servant entered the room and said, "Mistress, your father asks you to leave your books and help to decorate your sister's bedroom. You know that tomorrow is the wedding-day."

Bianca said, "Farewell, sweet tutors. I must be gone."

She and the servant exited.

Lucentio said, "Since Bianca is no longer here, I have no reason to stay."

He exited.

Hortensio, suspicious, said to himself, "But I have reason to investigate this pedant Cambio. I think that he looks as though he were in love. Bianca, if you are the type of girl to cast your wandering eyes on every low-born fellow who professes to love you, then I do not want you. If I ever catch you straying, then I will stray away from you and catch someone else."

It was the Sunday during which Petruchio and Katherina were supposed to be married, but Petruchio had not shown up. Baptista, Gremio, Tranio, Katherina, Bianca, Lucentio, and others were waiting for Petruchio to show up, and they were beginning to think that he had jilted the bride on her wedding day.

Baptista said to the disguised Tranio, whom of course he thought was Lucentio, "Signior Lucentio, this is the appointed day during which Katherina and Petruchio should be married, and yet we have not heard from our supposed-to-be son-in-law. What will people say? What mockery and gossip will occur because no bridegroom is here although the priest is ready to ask him if he takes Katherina to be his lawfully wedded wife? Lucentio, do you have anything to say about this shame of ours?"

Katherina interrupted and said, "It is no shame of ours because it is nobody's shame but mine. I have been, truly, forced to promise to marry — although my heart opposes it — a mad-brain rude lout who lacks all control. He deliberately wooed in haste and means to wed at leisure. I told you that he was a frantic fool, hiding his bitter jests in blunt behavior. He wants a reputation as a merry fellow, and so he woos a thousand women, appoints the day of marriage, makes feasts, invites friends, and announces the engagement — and he does not intend ever to wed those women whom he has wooed. Now the world will point at poor Katherina, and say, 'Look, there is mad Petruchio's wife — if he ever comes and marries her!'"

Tranio tried to comfort them: "Be patient, good Katherina, and Baptista, too. I swear by my life that Petruchio means only the best for you, despite whatever ill fortune is keeping him from keeping his word. Although Petruchio is blunt, I know that he is very wise. Although Petruchio is fond of merry jokes, I know that he is honorable."

Katherina said, "I wish that I had never seen him!"

Crying, she left. Bianca and some other women followed her.

Baptista said, "Go, girl. I cannot blame you for crying now for such an injury would vex even a saint, so no wonder it vexes a shrew of your hot temper."

Biondello ran up to Baptista and the others, shouting, "Baptista, I have news. I have old news that you have never heard before!"

"If I have never heard it before, it is new news," Baptista said. "How is it possible that you have new news and old news?"

"Why, is it not new news to hear of Petruchio's coming?" Biondello replied.

"Has he come?"

"Why, no, sir."

"What are you saying, then?"

"He is coming."

"When will he be here?"

"When he stands where I am and sees you there."

Tranio interrupted and said, "That is your new news. Now what is your old news?"

"Did I say *old* news? I meant to say *odd* news. Know that Petruchio is wearing lots of old and odd clothes, although he has a new hat. He is wearing an old jacket. He is wearing an old pair of pants that have been turned inside out because they have been worn so much. His boots are so old that they have been used to store pieces of candles — one boot is buckled, and the other boot is laced. He is carrying an old rusty sword taken out of the town-armory — the sword has a broken hilt and lacks a sheath. His garters are broken and do not hold up his stockings.

"His horse has an old moth-eaten saddle and stirrups that do not match. The horse's bit is broken, and the halter is made out of low-quality sheepskin instead of leather — the sheepskin has often been broken and then repaired with knots. The horse's girth strap has been repaired six times, and the horse's crupper — the strap that goes under the horse's tail and helps to steady the saddle — is made of velvet and bears studs that form the two initials of the woman who used to own it. Here and there packthread has been used to keep the whole setup from falling to pieces.

"As for Petruchio's horse, it has a dislocated hip, a swollen jaw, and diseases of the mouth. It has a runny nose. It staggers and has tumors on its fetlocks. It has swollen leg-joints and is yellow with jaundice. It has swellings behind the ears and is food for parasites. Its back sags, and a shoulder is dislocated. Finally, it is knock-kneed."

"Who is coming with Petruchio?" Baptista asked.

"Sir, his lackey, Grumio," Biondello said. "He is dressed up like the horse. He has a linen stocking on one leg and a woolen stocking on the other. He is using red and blue strips of cloth as his garters. His hat is old, and he has a weird ornament pinned on it instead of the usual feather. He is a monster, a true monster, in his choice of apparel — he is not like a Christian footboy or a gentleman's lackey."

Tranio said, "Some odd mood is making Petruchio act and dress like this, although he often dresses badly."

Baptista said, "I am glad that he has come, howsoever he comes."

Biondello said, "Why, sir, he comes not."

"Didn't you say that he is coming?"

"What? That Petruchio has come?"

"Yes, that Petruchio has come."

"No, sir," Biondello said. "I said that his horse is coming, with him on his back."

"Isn't that the same thing?" Baptista said.

Biondello sang, "*Nay, by Saint Jamy,*

"*I hold you a penny,*

"*A horse and a man*

"*Are more than one,*

"*And yet not many.*"

Petruchio and Grumio arrived, dressed as Biondello had described them.

"Come, where are these lads?" Petruchio shouted. "Who's at home?"

"You are welcome, sir," Baptista said.

"And yet I come not well," Petruchio replied.

"And yet you do not limp, so you have been well enough to come," Baptista said.

Tranio said to Petruchio, "If by come not well, you mean that you came here not well dressed, I agree with you. You are not dressed as well as I wish you were."

"Even if I were better dressed, I would still rush to be here," Petruchio said. "But where is Kate? Where is my lovely bride? How is my father? Gentlemen, it seems to me that you frown and are displeased. Why is everyone in this worthy group staring at me as if they saw some wondrous omen, some comet bringing a warning of upcoming disaster, or some unusual portent?"

Baptista replied, "Why, sir, you know this is your wedding-day. You have arrived late for your wedding. At first we were sad, fearing you would not come.

Now we are sadder because you have come so unprepared for your wedding. Change your clothing. What you are wearing is shameful and a disgrace to someone of your social class. What you are wearing is an eyesore, especially at a wedding!"

Tranio said, "Please tell us what important reason has made you arrive so late for your wedding and made you come here dressed like this? This is unlike yourself."

"The important reason is tedious to tell and harsh to hear," Petruchio said.

This is true, he thought. *I am late and badly dressed in order to out-shrew the shrew who will be my wife. She has made others uncomfortable with her shrewishness, and I will make her uncomfortable with my shrewishness. I intend to teach her how she has made other people feel so that she will reform her behavior. Once she has thoroughly learned that lesson, I will cast off my assumed behavior and be a husband whom she can be proud of.*

Petruchio added, "Let it be enough for now that I have come to keep my word to marry Kate even though I have been forced to change part of my plan — as you can see, I did not buy the new clothing I told you that I was planning to buy. When we have more leisure, I will explain myself and excuse my actions so well that you will be happy and satisfied with my explanation. But where is Kate? I have been too long away from her. The morning is passing, and it is time we were at church."

Tranio said, "Do not see your bride while you are wearing these disrespectable clothes. Go to my bedchamber, and put on some of my clothes."

"No," Petruchio said. "Believe me when I tell you that I will visit Kate while I am dressed like this."

Baptista said, "I trust that you will not marry her while you are dressed in these clothes."

"Indeed, I will marry her while I am dressed in these clothes," Petruchio said, "so talk no more about my clothing. She will be married to me — not to my clothes. I can change my clothing easily and make it better. Kate will soon wear out a certain part of my body in bed and if I could soon revive that part of my body — as soon as I can revive your opinion of my clothes by putting on different clothing — it will be good for Kate and better for me. But I am a fool to chat with you when I should bid good morning to my bride, and seal the title with a loving kiss! Very soon, she will bear the title of my wife."

Petruchio and Grumio exited.

Tranio said, "Petruchio has a reason to be dressed so madly. We will persuade him, if possible, to put on better clothing before he goes to church."

"I will follow him and see what happens," Baptista said.

Baptista, Gremio, and everyone except Tranio and Lucentio exited.

Tranio said, "You already have Bianca's love, but now we need her father's approval. To get her father's approval, as I explained previously to you, I must get a man — what kind of man does not matter because we can teach him to act the way he needs to act — to pretend to be your father, Vincentio of Pisa. He will promise Baptista that the dower for Bianca will consist of even greater sums than I have already promised. That way, you will get your wish and marry sweet Bianca with her father's consent."

Lucentio replied, "If my fellow tutor, Litio, were not watching Bianca's steps so closely, it would be a good idea, I think, for she and I to steal our marriage by eloping. Once the marriage has been performed, let all the world say no. I will keep the wife who is mine, no matter what all the world says."

"I will look into the possibility of your eloping," Tranio said. "We will outwit the greybeard Gremio; Bianca's watchful father, Baptista; and the crafty and amorous musician Litio. All of this we will do for your sake."

Gremio walked over to Tranio and Lucentio.

Tranio asked, "Signior Gremio, have you come from the church?"

"Yes, and as willingly as I ever came from school."

"Are the bride and bridegroom returning soon?"

"A bridegroom, you say? He is a groom indeed — he is like the groom who cleans a stable. He is a grumbling groom, and that is something that Katherina is quickly learning. He is even more ill tempered than she is."

"Even more ill tempered than Katherina?" Tranio said. "That is impossible."

"Why, he's a devil, a devil, a very fiend."

"Why, she's a devil, a devil, the devil's dam. She is the mother of the devil."

"Ha! She's a lamb, a dove, a harmless innocent compared to him!" Gremio said. "Let tell you, Sir Lucentio, about the wedding. When the priest asked him if he took Katherina as his wife, he replied, 'Yes, damn it!' He swore so loudly that the shocked priest dropped the Holy Bible. When he stooped to pick it up, Petruchio — that mad-brained bridegroom — hit him and made the priest and the Holy Bible fall again. Petruchio then said, 'Now help pick them up, if anyone wants to.'"

"What did Katherina say when the priest rose again?"

"She said nothing," Gremio replied. "All she did was tremble and shake because Petruchio stamped his feet and swore as if he thought that the vicar meant to cheat him in some way. But after all the religious rites were done, Petruchio called for wine: 'A toast!' He acted as if he were on board a ship, carousing with his mates after a storm. He chugged the wine and then threw the dregs in the sexton's face, giving as his reason that the sexton's beard grew thinly and seemed to require nourishment to grow thicker. This done, he took his bride, Katherina, about the neck and kissed her lips with such a loud smack that the church echoed. Seeing this, I left because I was embarrassed for Katherina. Coming after me, I know, the whole crowd of guests will soon arrive. Such a mad marriage as this has never been seen before."

At their church marriage, Petruchio and Katherina had made their vows before God. The vows had come from the 1559 Book of Common Prayer.

Petruchio had vowed before God, "I, Petruchio, take you, Katherina, to be my wedded wife, to have and to hold from this day forward, for better, for worse, for richer, for poorer, in sickness, and in health, **to love and to cherish**, until death do us part, according to God's holy ordinance, and I give you my true and faithful word to keep this vow."

Katherina had vowed before God, "I, Katherina, take you, Petruchio, to be my wedded husband, to have and to hold, from this day forward, for better, for worse, for richer, for poorer, in sickness, and in health, **to love, cherish, and obey**, until death do us part, according to God's holy ordinance, and I give you my true and faithful word to keep this vow."

Katherina had seemed to respect the wedding ceremony, and she had made the vow, but she did not seriously take the vow that she had made, as her actions would soon show. She had promised to love, honor, and obey her husband, but very quickly, she would refuse to do those things.

Petruchio had seemed to make a mockery of the wedding ceremony, but he had made the vow, and he seriously took the vows that he and Katherina had made, as his actions would soon show. If he did not love and cherish his wife, he would ignore her and allow her to continue to be a shrew, but he instead would take great pains to improve her character — she would become a wife who seriously took the vow she had made before God.

Gremio said, "Listen! I hear the minstrels playing. The bride, groom, and guests are coming."

As music played, Petruchio, Katherina, Bianca, Baptista, Hortensio, Grumio, and many other people, including guests, arrived.

Petruchio said, "Gentlemen and friends, I thank you for your pains in preparing this wedding. I know that you think to dine with me today, and I know that you have prepared a great wedding feast, but I need to leave quickly and so now I mean to take my leave."

"Is it possible you will go away tonight?" Baptista asked.

"I must go away today, before night comes," Petruchio said. "Don't be surprised; if you knew my business, you would beg me to go rather than to stay."

This is true, he thought. *My business is to tame my shrew of a wife and make her a good wife who will respect the vow she made before God.*

He added, "And, honest company, I thank you all. You have seen me give myself away to this most patient, sweet, and virtuous wife. Dine with my father, and drink a toast to me. I must leave, and so I say farewell to you all."

"Let us entreat you to stay until after dinner," Tranio said.

"I still must leave," Petruchio said.

"Let me entreat you," Gremio said.

"I still must leave," Petruchio said.

"Let me entreat you," Katherina said.

"I am content," Petruchio said.

"Are you content to stay?"

"I am content that you have entreated me to stay, but yet I will not stay, no matter how much you entreat me."

"If you love me, stay," Katherina said.

"Grumio, bring my horses," Petruchio said.

"Yes, sir, they are ready. The oats have eaten the horses."

"No," Katherina, who had just minutes ago vowed to obey her husband, said. "Do whatever you will, I will not go today. In fact, I will not go tomorrow. In fact, I will not go until it pleases me. The door is open, sir; there lies your way. Leave now, and you will start your journey with clean boots. As for me, I will not leave until it pleases me to leave. It is likely that you will prove to be an overbearing, surly bridegroom, since you are throwing your weight around so boldly."

Petruchio said, "Kate, be content. Please, do not be angry."

"I will be angry," Katherina said. "What business is it of yours?"

Anticipating an interruption, she said, "Father, be quiet. My husband will wait until I say it is time to leave."

Gremio anticipated a scene: "Now she'll get it!"

Katherina said, "Gentlemen, go to the bridal dinner. I see that a woman may be made a fool, if she lacks the spirit to resist."

Petruchio said, "They shall go to the bridal dinner, Kate, at your command."

He said to the guests, "Obey the bride, all of you who are celebrating her marriage. Go to the feast, revel and riot, carouse in full measure to celebrate the passing of her virginity. Be mad and be merry, or go hang yourselves. But as for my lovely Kate, she must go with me."

He added to the guests, and to Katherina, as he pretended that the guests were going to come between his wife and him, "No, do not defy me. Do not look offended; do not stamp your feet, or stare, or fret. I will be master of what is my own. She is my goods, my moveable possessions; she is my house, my household stuff, my field, my barn, my horse, my ox, my ass, my anything."

Petruchio knew the Bible well, including the Tenth Commandment: "*You shalt not covet your neighbor's house, you shalt not covet your neighbor's wife, nor his manservant, nor his maidservant, nor his ox, nor his ass, nor anything that is your neighbor's.*"

Petruchio said, "Here my wife stands. If anyone dares to touch her, I will bring a legal action against even the proudest man who tries to stop me from leaving Padua and taking my wife with me. Grumio, draw your weapon, for we are beset by thieves. Rescue your mistress, if you are a man."

He pretended that his wife was afraid that the wedding guests were going to keep her from joining her husband: "Fear not, sweet wench. They shall not touch you, Kate. I will shield you against a million like them."

He carried her away as Grumio "protected" them with his drawn but broken sword.

Baptista watched them leave, realized that his daughter had already broken her promise to obey her husband, remembered that he hoped that Petruchio would be the right husband — a husband who could tame her and whom she could respect — for his shrewish daughter, and said, "Let them go. They are certainly a 'quiet' and 'peaceful' couple."

Gremio said, "If they had not left so quickly, I would have died from laughing so much."

"Of all mad matches, this is the maddest," Tranio said.

Lucentio asked Bianca, "What is your opinion of your sister and her marriage?"

"I believe that, being mad herself, she is madly mated."

Gremio said, "In my opinion, Petruchio is Kated. Either they are equally matched, or one of them has met his match. Either way, Petruchio is mated with Kate."

Baptista said, "Neighbors and friends, although the bride and bridegroom will not be eating with us, you know that we have no lack of delicacies at the feast."

He added, "Lucentio, you shall sit in the bridegroom's seat and Bianca shall take her sister's seat."

Tranio asked, "Shall sweet Bianca practice how to bride it?"

"She shall, Lucentio," Baptista replied. "Come, gentlemen, let's go."

CHAPTER 4

— 4.1 —

Grumio entered Petruchio's house in Verona and said, "Damn all weak and ill-conditioned horses! Damn all mad masters! Damn all bad roads! Was ever a man as beaten as I am? Was ever a man so dirty? Was ever a man so tired? I have been sent ahead of my master and his wife to make a fire; they will soon be here and will need to warm themselves. I am freezing, although I am a little pot and soon hot — although I am short, I get angry quickly and so warm up. If this were not true, I am so cold that my lips might freeze to my teeth and my tongue might freeze to the roof of my mouth, and my heart might freeze in my chest before I should come by a fire to thaw me. I will warm myself by fanning the embers. It is a good thing that I am short — a taller man than I am would catch cold."

With a voice that quivered because he was shivering, Grumio shouted for a servant, "Curtis!"

Curtis walked into the room and asked, "Who is it who calls so coldly?"

"A piece of ice," Grumio replied, "If you doubt that I am a piece of ice, you may slide from my shoulder to my heel with no greater a running start than my head and my neck. Start a fire, good Curtis."

"Are my master and his wife coming, Grumio?"

"Yes, Curtis, yes, and therefore start a fire. An old song says, '*Scotland's burning ... Fire, fire! Cast on water*,' but throw no water on this fire because I need it badly to keep from freezing."

Curtis started making a fire in a fireplace.

"Is my master's wife as hot a shrew as she's reported to be?" Curtis asked.

"She was, good Curtis, before this frost," Grumio replied, "but, as you know, winter tames man, woman, and beast. It has tamed my old master and my new mistress and myself, fellow Curtis."

"You may be a beast, but I am not," Curtis said. "Do not call me your fellow since you have just admitted that you are a beast. Go away, you three-inch fool!"

"Is what is mine only three inches long?" Grumio said, "Why, the horn on your head that identifies you as a man with an unfaithful wife is a foot long.

What I have between my legs is at least that long. But will you make a fire, or shall I complain about you to our mistress, whose hand, now that she is close at hand, you shall soon feel, to your cold comfort, for being slow in your hot office? Do your job, and make a fire."

"Good Grumio, tell me, how goes the world? What's the news?"

"The world is cold," Grumio said, "for everyone but you, who has the job of making fires, so do your duty, and take what is due to you, because my master and mistress are almost frozen to death. Petruchio and Katherina are, like me, cold."

"The fire is ready," Curtis said. "Therefore, Grumio, tell me the news."

Grumio sang, "Jack, boy! Ho, boy!"

Then he added, "Before I can tell you anything, the news must thaw."

"Come, you are so full of trickery! You must be a master at trapping rabbits!"

"Make the fire bigger because I have caught extreme cold," Grumio said. "Where's the cook? Is supper ready? Is the house tidied? Are the rushes strewn on the floor? Are the cobwebs swept away? Are the serving men wearing their new livery and their white stockings? Does every upper servant have his wedding token on? Are all the male and female servants ready and the big and little glasses, too? Are the tablecloths on the tables, and is everything in order?"

"All is ready; and therefore, please, please tell me the news. What happened during your journey?"

"First, know that my horse is tired," Grumio said, "and know that my master and mistress have fallen out."

"How?"

"They have fallen out of their saddles into the dirt; and thereby hangs a tale."

"Let us hear the tale, good Grumio."

"Lend me your ear."

"Here it is," Curtis said, inclining an ear toward Grumio, who hit it.

"You are making me feel a tale, not hear a tale," Curtis said.

"And therefore it is called a sensible tale because you are able to sense it," Grumio said. "I knocked at your ear to wake it up and beg it to listen. Now I begin my tale: *Imprimis* — that is legal talk for 'first of all' — we came down a foul hill, my master, Petruchio, riding behind my mistress, Katherina."

"Were both riding on one horse?"

"What is the difference?"

"Why, the difference of a horse."

"You should tell the tale since you are going to keep interrupting," Grumio said. "If you had not interrupted me, you would have heard how Katherina's horse fell and she fell under her horse. You would have heard in how muddy a place she fell, how she was covered in mud, how he left her with the horse over her, how he beat *me* because *her* horse stumbled, how she waded through the dirt to pluck him off me, how he swore, how she prayed — this woman who never prayed before — how I cried, how the horses ran away, how her bridle was broken, how I lost my crupper — that strap that goes under the horse's tail and keeps the saddle steady — with many other things worth recording, which now shall die in oblivion due to being untold, resulting in you returning unenlightened to your grave."

"According to your tale, Petruchio is more of a shrew than his wife."

"Yes, he is," Grumio said, "and you and the proudest of you all shall find that to be true when he comes home. But why am I talking about this? Call forth Nathaniel, Joseph, Nicholas, Philip, Walter, Sugarsop, and the rest. Let their heads be sleekly combed, their servants' blue coats brushed, and their garters be matched. Let them curtsy with their left legs and not presume to touch a hair of my master's horse's tail until they have kissed their master's and their mistress' hands in greeting. Are they all ready?"

"They are."

"Call them forth."

Curtis shouted, "Did you hear?"

Some servants were eavesdropping.

Curtis shouted, "You must meet my master to countenance — to pay respect to — my mistress."

"To countenance?" Grumio, who was always willing and happy to deliberately misinterpret words, said. "Why, she has a face of her own."

"Who does not know that?"

"Apparently, you — you are the one calling for company to countenance her."

"I call them forth to credit her — to pay respect to her, to honor her," Curtis said.

"To credit her? Why, she has not come to borrow something from them."

Some servants entered the room.

Nathaniel said, "Welcome home, Grumio!"

Philip asked, "How are you, Grumio?"

Joseph said, "Hey, Grumio!"

Nicholas said, "Grumio, my friend!"

Nathaniel asked, "How are you, old lad?"

Grumio said to the four servants, "Welcome, you ... how are you now? ... hey, you ... my friend, you."

Then he added, "So much for my greetings. Now, my fine fellows, is everything ready, and are all things tidy?"

Nathaniel replied, "All things are ready. How near is our master?"

"Very close indeed," Grumio said. "By this time, he has dismounted. Therefore, you must — quiet! I hear him coming!"

Petruchio and Katherina entered the room. Katherina went directly to the fire.

"Where are these knaves?" Petruchio shouted. "What, no servant at my door to hold my stirrup or to take my horse! Where are Nathaniel, Gregory, Philip?"

Nathaniel said, "Here, sir."

Gregory said, "Here, sir."

Philip said, "Here, sir."

Petruchio shouted, "Here, sir! Here, sir! Here, sir! You logger-headed and unpolished servants! What, you can't be bothered to show up to do your work? You can't be bothered to show respect to me? You can't be bothered to obey me? Will no one do his duty? Where is the foolish knave I sent here before me?"

Grumio replied, "Here I am, sir — I am just as foolish as I was before."

Petruchio shouted at him, "You peasant country bumpkin! You son of a whore! You are as much of a mindless drudge as a horse that turns a treadmill to grind barley to make malt! Didn't I order you to meet me outside and bring along these rascal knaves with you?"

Grumio replied with several ridiculous excuses: "Nathaniel's coat, sir, was not fully made. Gabriel's shoes needed to be repaired. Peter's hat was not darkened because no smoky torch could be found. Walter had not yet found a sheath for his dagger. No one was properly dressed except for Adam, Ralph, and Gregory. All the rest were ragged, old, and beggarly. Yet, dressed as they are, they have come here to meet you."

Petruchio said, "Go, rascals, go, and fetch my supper."

The servants exited.

Petruchio sang, "*Where is the life that late I led —*"

He stopped singing and began to say, "Where are those —"

Then he interrupted himself and said, "Sit down, Kate, and welcome."

He began to bang on the table and shout, "Food! Food! Food! Food!"

The servants arrived with the meal and began to place it on a serving table near the dining table at which Petruchio and Katherina were sitting.

Petruchio shouted at the servants, "Hurry!"

He said to his wife, "Don't look sad, Kate. Be merry."

To the servants, he shouted, "Take off my boots! Hurry!"

Part of Petruchio's plan was to outshrew the shrew and by so doing show her how her shrewish and inconsiderate actions affected other people. This part of his plan was succeeding.

He sang, "*It was the friar of orders grey,*

"*As he walked forth on his way —*"

He shouted at a servant who was trying to pull off one of his boots, "Get out, rogue! You are twisting my ankle! You better do a better job with the other boot! Take that!"

He hit the servant.

He said, "Be merry, Kate."

He shouted, "Bring some water here!

"Where's Troilus, my cocker spaniel?

"Get you hence, and order my cousin Ferdinand to come hither. He is one, Kate, whom you must kiss, and be acquainted with.

"Where are my slippers?

"Bring me some water!"

A servant entered, carrying water.

Petruchio said, "Come, Kate, and wash your hands, and welcome heartily."

The servant dropped the water, and Petruchio shouted, "You son of a whore! You villain! Will you let it fall?"

Petruchio hit the servant who had dropped the water.

"Have patience, please," Katherina said. "He did not do it on purpose."

Katherina was learning about kindness and forgiveness and about feeling sympathy for other people. She was learning how shrewish behavior affected other people.

Petruchio said, "He is the son of a whore! He is a beetle-headed, flap-eared knave!"

He added, "Come, Kate, sit down. I know that you are hungry. Will you give thanks to God, sweet Kate; or else shall I?"

He asked a servant, "What is this? Mutton?"

The servant replied, "Yes."

"Who brought it?"

The servant Peter replied, "I did."

"This mutton is burnt, and so is all the food. What dogs are these servants! Where is the rascal cook? How dare you, villains, bring this food and serve it like this to me who hates burnt mutton and burnt food! Take it away!"

He swept the food and the dishes off the table and shouted, "You heedless joltheads and unmannered slaves! What, are you servants grumbling and complaining? I'll set you straight right away!"

"Please, husband," Katherina said. "The food was fine. You need not be so picky."

"I tell you, Kate, it was burnt and dried up, and I am expressly forbidden to touch it because overcooked food makes people hot-headed and angry. It is better that both of us fast rather than eat it because both of us have quick tempers. Be patient. Tomorrow this fault will be corrected, and we will have good food to eat. Tonight, however, both of us will go without food. Come, I will take you to your bridal chamber."

Petruchio and Katherina exited, and the servants began to talk.

Nathaniel asked, "Peter, did you ever see the like of that?"

"Petruchio is beating her at her game. She is hot-headed, but he is pretending to be even more hot-headed than she is. He is giving her a taste of her own medicine."

Curtis came into the room.

Grumio asked, "Where is Petruchio?"

Curtis replied, "He is in her bedchamber, talking to her about self-control. In his sermon to her, he shouts, and swears, and scolds, so that she, poor soul, does not know which way to stand, to look, or to speak. She sits dazed as if she has newly awakened from a dream."

Curtis heard a noise and said, "Let's go now! I hear Petruchio coming!"

The servants left quickly.

Petruchio walked into the room and started to think out loud:

"I have started my reign with cunning, and I hope that my carefully thought-out plan will succeed.

"We train falcons to obey their masters by keeping them very hungry, and I will keep Kate very hungry. I will not allow her to eat her fill until she fulfills the vow she made before God to love, honor, and obey me.

"To train a hawk, and have it obey the call of her master, the trainer must watch the hawk until it is trained. Untrained hawks will be enraged and will beat their wings in frustration and will not be obedient.

"Kate ate no food today, and I will not allow her to eat tonight. Last night she did not sleep, and tonight I will not allow her to sleep. I pretended to find fault with the food, and I will pretend to find fault with the bed. I will fling the pillow there, I will fling the cushion here, I will fling the coverlet this way, and I will fling the sheets another way.

"While I do these things, I will tell her that everything I do is done in reverend care of her — and that is true, if it gets rid of her shrewishness, as I intend it will.

"Kate shall stay awake all night. And if she begins to nod and go to sleep, I'll shout and brawl and with the clamor keep her always awake.

"This is a way to kill a wife with kindness.

"By doing these things, I will curb her mad and headstrong shrewishness. Once she is tamed, I will be a proper husband to her. I will love and cherish her. I do, already, although it may not seem like it.

"If anyone knows better how to tame a shrew, I want to hear from him his better way. His telling everyone the secret would be a service to the world."

Tranio and Hortensio were speaking in front of Baptista's house. Tranio was still disguised as his master, Lucentio, and Hortensio was still disguised as the tutor Litio. Hortensio had been spying on Bianca and was convinced that she and the tutor Cambio — who was really Lucentio in disguise, although Hortensio did not know that — were in love.

Tranio said, "Is it really possible, friend Litio, that Mistress Bianca fancies any one other than me, Lucentio? I tell you, sir, she seems to treat me encouragingly, although you say that she is completely deceiving me. Is she really leading me on?"

"Sir, to satisfy you that what I have said is true," Hortensio replied, "stand hidden here and watch the interaction of tutor Cambio and student Bianca."

Lucentio and Bianca walked into the garden for a lesson.

Lucentio asked, "Bianca, have you learned anything from what you have read?"

"Which book are you reading? Answer me that first," Bianca said.

"I am reading a book whose advice I follow: Ovid's *The Art of Love*."

Lucentio thought, *It is a manual on how to seduce women.*

Bianca said, "I hope that you are a master in that art."

"And I hope that you will prove to be the mistress of my heart!"

Hortensio said, "They are fast learners! What do you think? Do you still think that Bianca loves no one except for you?"

"Bianca's 'love' for me has been deceiving and deceitful," Tranio said. "Women are unfaithful. What I have seen here is incredible, Litio."

Hortensio decided to reveal his true identity: "Be mistaken no more. I am not Litio. I am Hortensio, who disguised myself as a music tutor to be close to Bianca and woo her. But I am ashamed that I have acted in this way. Bianca is not worthy of my wooing her. She prefers a low-born man like Cambio to a gentleman of high birth like me. She loves a peasant. She does not love me."

Tranio replied, "Signior Hortensio, I have often heard that you loved Bianca with all your heart. My eyes are now witnesses of her unworthiness and unfaithfulness. I am ready — like you — to stop wooing Bianca. Do you approve of my decision?"

"Look at how they kiss and court each other!" Hortensio said. "I do approve of your decision. Let's shake on it. Here and now I firmly vow never to woo Bianca — I do give her up because she is unworthy of all the former favors that I have previously given to her."

"And here I take the unfeigned oath that I will never marry her even if she begs me to," Tranio said. "To Hell with her! Look at how unashamedly she pursues him!"

"I wish that everyone would vow not to marry Bianca so that she would be forced to marry her penniless tutor or be an old maid," Hortensio said. "To help ensure that I keep my oath, I will be married to a wealthy widow before three days have passed. This widow has loved me as long as I have loved this proud and disdainful Bianca. And so farewell, Signior Lucentio. Kindness in women, not their beauteous looks, shall win my love, and so I take my leave. I will keep the vow that I have made and you have witnessed."

He exited.

Tranio, of course, was happy that Hortensio had decided to marry a wealthy widow rather than Bianca. Hortensio was now one less rival suitor to Bianca, and his withdrawal made it more likely that the real Lucentio would succeed in marrying Bianca.

Tranio went over to Lucentio and Bianca and said, "Mistress Bianca, may God bless you with such happiness as belongs to a lover. I have caught you two courting, and both Hortensio and I have sworn not to marry you."

"Tranio, are you joking?" Bianca said. "Has Hortensio really sworn not to marry me?"

"Bianca, we have both sworn not to marry you."

Lucentio had figured out that the tutor Litio was really Hortensio in disguise. He said, "Then we are rid of Litio."

"Yes, you are," Tranio said. "He said that he will marry a merry widow. He intends to woo and wed her quickly."

"May God give him joy!" Bianca said.

"Hortensio will tame the widow," Tranio said.

"He *says* that he will, Tranio," Bianca replied.

"Indeed, he has gone to the taming-school."

"The taming-school?" Bianca said. "Is there really such a place?"

"Yes, there is," Tranio said, "and Petruchio is the schoolmaster. He teaches the right tricks for taming a shrew and her chattering tongue. Hortensio has gone to visit Petruchio in Verona."

Lucentio's other servant, Biondello, arrived and said, "Master, I have been on the lookout so long for a man who will pretend to be your father that I am dog-weary, but at last I have spied a Heaven-sent old man coming down the hill. He is the right kind of man to pretend to be your father."

"What is he like, Biondello?" Lucentio asked.

"Master, he is a merchant or perhaps a pedant, I do not know for sure, but his clothing, walk, and appearance are like those of a father."

"What do we do now, Tranio?" Lucentio asked.

"If he is credulous and trusts the tale I will tell him," Tranio said, "I will make him glad to pretend to be your father, Vincentio, and to make promises to Baptista Minola about the dower that I — while pretending to be you — have promised for Bianca. He will pass as your father. Now you and Bianca go inside and leave me alone to talk to him."

Lucentio and Bianca went inside.

The old man arrived, walking on the street outside Baptista's house.

The old man saw Tranio and greeted him, "God bless you, sir!"

Tranio walked over to the old man and said, "And may God bless you, sir! You are welcome. Do you have far to travel, or have you reached your destination?"

"I will stay here for a week or two, but then I will travel farther. I will go to Rome and then to Tripoli, if God permits."

"Where are you from, please?"

"I am from Mantua."

"From Mantua, sir!" Tranio pretended to be shocked. "God forbid! Why have you come to Padua, where your life is in danger?"

"My life is in danger!" the old man said. "That is hard news! Why is my life in danger?"

"It is death for anyone in Mantua to come to Padua," Tranio said. "Don't you know the cause? The Duke of Padua, who is quarreling with the Duke of Mantua, has ordered all Mantuan ships to be detained in Venice. News of the Dukes' quarrel has spread widely. It is a marvel that you have not yet heard about it, but then you are newly arrived in Padua. Otherwise, you would have heard about it."

"This is extremely bad news for me," the old man said. "For I have promissory notes from Florence that I must exchange here for cash."

"Well, sir, I will do you a favor and also give you advice," Tranio said. "First, tell me, have you ever been in Pisa?"

"Yes, sir," the old man said. "I have often been in Pisa, which is renowned for grave and wise citizens."

"Among these grave and wise citizens, do you know a certain Vincentio?"

"I do not know him personally, but I have heard of him," the old man said. "He is a merchant of immense wealth."

"He is my father, sir," Tranio lied, "and, it is true to say, in appearance he somewhat resembles you."

Biondello thought, *Vincentio and this old man resemble each other as much as do an apple and an oyster, but that hardly matters.*

"To save your life in these extremely dangerous circumstances, I will do you a favor for my father's sake. It is fortunate that you resemble Vincentio because you can pretend to be him and assume his name and reputation. You will safely stay in my house. Just be careful to stay in character as my father — that is important. That way, you can stay in Padua until you have finished your business here. If you wish to accept my kind offer, you are welcome to do so."

"Sir, I do accept your kind offer," the old man said. "For ever after, I will consider you the savior of my life and liberty."

"Then go with me and we will put this plan in action," Tranio said. "As we walk, let me give you information. My father is expected here any day now to make a formal agreement about a dower in marriage — I will be married to one of the daughters of a certain Baptista here. I will teach you what to say and what to do, and I will dress you in clothing that will suit the role you will play."

In a room of Petruchio's house, a very hungry Katherina was attempting to get the servant Grumio to bring her food. This attempt was doomed to be unsuccessful because Grumio was obeying the instructions of Petruchio, part of whose plan to tame the shrewish Katherina was to keep food away from her.

"No, I will not bring you food," Grumio said. "If I were to get caught, Petruchio would kill me."

"The greater the wrong he does to me, the more spiteful Petruchio becomes," Katherina said. "Did he marry me in order to starve me? Beggars who come to my father's door and ask for food are immediately given a meal. If they are not, they are given charity elsewhere. But I, who have never learned how to beg, and who have never needed to beg, am starved for lack of food and giddy for lack of sleep. I am kept awake by loud oaths and fed with brawling. And what vexes me more than all these things is that he says that he does these things because he loves me with a perfect love. It is as if he believes that if I should sleep or eat, then I would get a deadly sickness or die immediately. Please go and get me something to eat. I don't care what you get me, as long as it is wholesome food."

"What do you say to a cooked calf's foot?" Grumio asked.

"It is very good. Please let me have it."

"I fear that it is a food that causes ill temper," Grumio said. "What do you say to a fat tripe finely broiled?"

"I like it well. Good Grumio, bring me one."

"I don't know. I am afraid that it would cause you to be ill tempered. What do you say to a piece of beef and mustard?"

"It is a dish that I love to eat."

"True, but the mustard is a little too hot."

"Then bring me the beef without the mustard."

"No, I will not," Grumio said. "You shall have mustard, or else you get no beef from Grumio."

"Then bring me both, or just one of them, or any kind of food at all."

"Why then, I will bring you the mustard without the beef."

"Get away from me," Katherina said, hitting Grumio. "You are a false deluding slave who feeds me only with words and not with food. May God bring sorrow upon you and all the pack of you who triumph and feel glad because I am miserable. Get out!"

Petruchio and Hortensio, who was visiting Petruchio, came into the room. They were carrying food.

"How are you, my Kate?" Petruchio said. "What, sweetie, are you depressed?"

Hortensio asked, "How are you?"

"I am cold because I have met with cold cheer," Katherina replied.

"Pluck up your spirits, and look cheerfully upon me," Petruchio said. "Here, love. You can see how diligent I am to fix this food myself and bring it to you. I am sure, sweet Kate, that this kindness merits thanks. What, not a word of thanks? I can see that you do not want this food and therefore I went to all this trouble for nothing. I see that I need to have this food taken away."

"Please, let the food stay here," Katherina said.

"The smallest service is repaid with thanks, and so shall my service be repaid before you touch the food."

"I thank you, sir," Katherina said.

"Signior Petruchio, you are to blame for Kate's poor spirits," Hortensio said. "Come, mistress Kate, I'll join you for your meal."

Petruchio was willing for Kate and him to go hungry, but he was not willing for a guest to go hungry, especially when the guest could help him in his plan to tame Katherina.

He whispered, "Do me a favor, Hortensio, and eat all the food. Do not let Kate have any of it."

Petruchio said loudly, "Hortensio, may your courtesy do your gentle heart good! Kate, eat quickly. My honey love, we will return to your father's house and enjoy ourselves while dressed as splendidly as the others there. We will have silken coats and hats and golden rings, with ruffs and cuffs and hooped skirts and things, with scarfs and fans and double change of fine clothing, with amber bracelets, beads, and lots of other girly things."

As Petruchio talked, Hortensio ate most of the food. Kate got very little — Petruchio and Hortensio made sure of that.

Petruchio said, "Are you finished eating? The tailor is waiting for you. He will adorn your body with his finery and ruffles."

The tailor entered the room, and Petruchio said, "Come, tailor, let us see these ornaments. Let us see the dress that you have made. Lay it out so we can see it."

A hat maker also entered the room, and Petruchio asked, "What business have you here?"

The hat maker replied, "Here is the hat your worship ordered."

Petruchio looked at the hat and pretended to dislike it.

He said, "Why, this was molded on a porridge bowl! It is a velvet dish! It is cheap and nasty! Why, it is a mollusk shell or a walnut shell. It is a knick-knack, a trifle, a piece of nonsense, a baby's hat. Take it away! Come, let me have a bigger hat!"

Katherina said, "I will have no bigger hat. This size is fashionable, and gentlewomen wear such hats as these."

Petruchio replied, "When you are gentle, you shall have one, too — but not until then."

Hortensio thought, *That will not be any time soon.*

Katherina said, "Why, sir, I trust I may have permission to speak, and speak I will. I am no child. I am no babe. Your betters have endured hearing me say my mind, and if you cannot endure it, it is best that you stop your ears. My tongue will tell the anger that is in my heart — if I keep that anger hidden, my heart will break. Rather than have it break, I will speak as freely as I want, even if what I have to say is extreme."

Petruchio pretended that Katherina had agreed with him that the hat was bad: "Why, what you say is true. This is a paltry hat, a custard-coffin — a crust for a custard — a bauble, a silken meat pie. I love you and your taste in hats — you hate this hat."

"Whether you love me or love me not, I like the hat. And I will have it, or I will have none."

Petruchio motioned for the hat maker to leave, and the hat maker obeyed.

The tailor had laid out the dress for inspection.

Petruchio said, "Let us look at the dress. Tailor, show it to us."

Petruchio looked at the dress and pretended not to like it: "Have mercy, God! What kind of fancy dress is this? What's this? A sleeve? It is like a small cannon. I see that you have pricked it open all over like an apple-tart. Here's a snip and a nip and a cut and a slish and a slash — these holes resemble an incense-burner with a perforated top in a barber's shop. Why, what in the devil's name, tailor, do you call this?"

Hortensio thought, *I can see that Kate is also not likely to have a new dress.*

"You wanted me to make the dress properly and well, according to the fashion of this time," the tailor said.

"So I did," Petruchio said, "but if you remembered, I did not order you to spoil it for all time. Leave here and pass every street gutter as you hop off to your home. For you shall hop off without any business from me, sir. I want none of the clothing you make. Go now! Take this dress and do whatever you want with it!"

Katherina said to Petruchio, "I have never seen a better-fashioned dress. I have never seen a dress that is more elegant, more pleasing, or more commendable. Are you trying to make a puppet — an easily manipulated doll — out of me?"

Petruchio pretended that she was talking about the tailor: "Why, that is true; the tailor is trying to make a puppet out of you."

The tailor replied, "She says that *you* intend to make a puppet out of her."

"Oh, monstrous arrogance!" Petruchio said. "You lie, you thread, you thimble — you are a yard, three-quarters of a yard, a half-yard, a quarter of a yard, one-sixteenth of a yard! You are a flea, a nit, a thin-legged insect! Am I to be defied in my own house by a spool of thread? Get out, you rag, you fragment, you remnant, or I shall so beat you with your yardstick that for the rest of your life you will think twice before prattling on this way. I tell you that you have ruined her dress."

"You are deceived," the tailor said. "The dress has been made according to the order given to my boss. Grumio gave us the order about how it should be done."

"I gave him no order; I gave him the fabric," Grumio said.

"But how did you want the dress to be made?" the tailor asked.

"Sir, with needle and thread," Grumio replied.

"But did you not request that the fabric be cut?"

"You have bedecked many things, haven't you?" Grumio asked.

"Yes, I have decorated many dresses with trimmings," the tailor said.

"Well, do not try to bedeck me. I will not be decked in a fight," Grumio said, "no matter how many men you have decked. I will not stand for it! I asked your boss to cut out the dress, but I did not ask him to cut it to pieces; therefore, you lie."

"I have right here the written order for the dress," the tailor said. "It tells in what fashion the dress should be made."

"Read it out loud," Petruchio ordered.

"The note lies if it says that I ordered the dress to be cut to pieces," Grumio said.

The tailor read out loud, "*First, a loose-bodied dress —*"

Grumio objected, "A loose-bodied dress! That is a dress for a woman with a loose body — a loose woman! Master, if ever I said loose-bodied dress, sew me in the skirts of it, and beat me to death with a bobbin of brown thread. I said a dress, not a loose-bodied dress."

"Proceed," Petruchio ordered.

The tailor read, "*With a small compassed cape.*"

"I confess that I ordered the cape," Grumio said.

"*With a wide sleeve*," the tailor read.

"I confess that I ordered two sleeves," Grumio said.

"The sleeves elaborately cut," the tailor read.

"There is the villainy — there is the problem," Petruchio said.

"There is an error in the order, sir," Grumio said. "I ordered that the sleeves should be cut out and then sewed up again. I will prove it in combat even though the tailor arms his little finger with a thimble."

"Everything that I have read is true," the tailor said. "If I had you in the right place — a court of law — the judge would agree with me, and not with you."

"I am ready to fight you now," Grumio said. "You take the order form, I will take your yardstick, and let us fight each other without mercy. You have no need to hold back when you fight me."

"May God have mercy," Hortensio said. "The tailor won't have a chance if he is armed only with a piece of paper."

"Well, sir, in brief, the dress is not for me," Petruchio said to the tailor. "I do not want it."

"You are in the right, sir," Grumio said. "It is for my mistress — your wife."

"Take the dress back to your boss and let him do what he wants with it," Petruchio said to the tailor. "Take it away for your master's use."

"Isn't that dirty?" Grumio asked.

"What do you mean?" Petruchio asked.

"You want this tailor to take away the dress for his master's use. That sounds like you want him to take the dress off a woman so that his master can use her," Grumio replied. "I am shocked!"

Petruchio ignored Grumio's coarse jesting and whispered, "Hortensio, say that you will see that the tailor will be paid."

To the tailor, Petruchio said, "Go and take the dress away. Be gone, and say no more."

Hortensio whispered to the tailor, "Do not worry. I'll pay you for the dress tomorrow. Do not be offended by Petruchio's rash and inconsiderate words. Go now, and send my regards to your boss."

The tailor exited.

Petruchio said, "Well, come, my Kate; we will go to your father's house wearing these respectable everyday clothes. Our purses shall be rich because we have not spent our money, and our garments will be poor. Our minds are more important than our bodies, and a rich mind will adorn the body. Just like the Sun breaks through the darkest clouds, honor can be seen through the meanest clothing. Is the loudly chattering blue jay more precious than the beautifully singing but plainly adorned morning lark because its feathers are more beautiful? Or is the poisonous adder better than the tasty eel because its patterned skin pleases the eye? Of course not, good Kate. And you are not the worse for this poor and mean clothing. If you consider your clothing to be shameful, blame it on me. I believe that quality of character is all and quality of clothing is nothing. And therefore let us be merry. We will leave immediately and go to your father's house to feast and be entertained."

He ordered a servant, "Go, call my men, and let us go straight to Kate's father. Bring our horses to the end of Long Lane. We will walk there and mount our horses. Let's see, I think it is now around seven o'clock, and we will probably arrive at Kate's father's house by dinnertime."

"I do assure you, sir, that it is almost two o'clock," Katherina said. "And it will be suppertime before we arrive there."

Petruchio replied, "It shall be seven or I will not mount my horse. Look, Kate, whatever I speak, or do, or think to do, you are always saying that I am wrong."

He told his servants, "Forget it. I will not go to Kate's father's house today; and before I do, it shall be whatever o'clock I say it is."

Hortensio thought, *Why, Petruchio intends to command the Sun to be whatever o'clock he says it is.*

Tranio and the old man, who was now dressed like Vincentio, Lucentio's father, talked together in front of Baptista's house. The old man was wearing boots and was bareheaded to make it seem as if he had just arrived from a journey.

Tranio said, "Sir, this is Baptista's house. Do you want me to ring his bell?"

"Of course, what else?" the old man said. "But unless I am deceived, Signior Baptista may remember me. Nearly twenty years ago, in Genoa, we met when we were lodgers at the Pegasus Inn."

"All will be well," Tranio said. "Keep in character no matter what happens. Be sure to have the gravitas that a father should have."

"I will," the old man said.

Biondello arrived.

The old man said, "But, sir, here comes your servant. It is a good idea for him to know what we are doing."

"Do not worry about him," Tranio said.

He added, "Biondello, now do your duty thoroughly, I advise you. Pretend that this man is the real Vincentio."

"I will. Don't worry," Biondello said.

"Did you take my message to Baptista?" Tranio asked.

"I told him that your father was at Venice, and that you expected him to arrive today in Padua."

"You are a good fellow," Tranio said. "Here, take this money and buy yourself a drink later."

He looked up and said, "Here comes Baptista. Old man, get ready."

Baptista and Lucentio walked over to Tranio, the old man, and Biondello.

Tranio said, "Signior Baptista, you are happily met."

He said to the old man who was pretending to be Lucentio's father, "Sir, this is the gentleman I told you about. I hope that you will be a good father to me now. Give me Bianca as and for my inheritance."

"Steady, son!" the old man said.

To Baptista, the old man said, "Sir, by your leave. I have come to Padua to collect some debts, and my son Lucentio has told me about an important matter: Your daughter and he love each other. Because of the good reports that

I have heard about you and because my son loves your daughter and she loves him, I am willing, as a loving father should be, to allow my son to be married right away. If you like this match of your daughter and my son as much as I do, then we can come to a financial agreement and together consent to this marriage. I will not try to drive a hard bargain with you, Baptista — I have heard many good things about you."

"Sir, pardon me for what I have to say," Baptista said. "Your plain-spokenness and your brevity well please me. It is true that your son Lucentio here loves my daughter and she loves him — or both are putting on quite an act! Therefore, as long as you assure me that like a good father who wants his son to be happy you will give my daughter a sufficient dower, the match is made and all is done. Your son shall marry my daughter with my consent."

"I thank you, sir," Tranio said. "Where then do you know that your daughter and I can best be formally engaged and the proper financial agreements be drawn up?"

"Not in my house, Lucentio," Baptista said, "for, you know, pitchers have ears, and I have many servants. Besides, old Gremio is always listening so perhaps we may be interrupted."

"Then we will do these things at my lodging, if it pleases you," Tranio said. "There, my father is staying; and there, this night, we will settle this business privately and well. Send for your daughter by your servant Cambio here. My servant Biondello shall fetch the notary at once to write out the financial agreements. The worst thing is that with so little notice, you are likely to have a thin and slender meal at my lodging."

"That is fine," Baptista said. "Cambio, go to my home and tell Bianca to get herself ready immediately. Please tell her what has happened: Lucentio's father has arrived in Padua, and she is likely to become Lucentio's wife."

Lucentio, disguised as Cambio, exited. As he did, Tranio winked at him and laughed.

"I pray to the gods that she will become Lucentio's wife with all my heart!" Biondello said.

"Dally not with the gods, but leave now," Tranio said.

Biondello exited. He had a message that Tranio wanted him to give to Lucentio.

Tranio said, "Signior Baptista, shall I lead the way? Welcome! A single course will most likely be all the food you receive at my lodging here, but we will do better in Pisa."

"I will follow you," Baptista said.

Tranio, the old man, and Baptista exited.

Biondello, meanwhile, shouted, "Cambio!"

Lucentio, still disguised as Cambio, walked over to him and said, "What do you want, Biondello?"

"Did you see my master wink and laugh?"

"Yes, Biondello, but what of that?"

"In themselves, nothing, but he has left me here behind to tell you the meaning of his wink and laugh."

"Please tell me their meaning."

"Baptista is safely away from you; he is talking with the pretend father of a pretend son."

"What about him?"

"You are supposed to bring his daughter to the supper."

"And what of it?"

"The old priest of Saint Luke's church is on duty at all hours."

"And what does this have to do with me?"

"While Baptista is busy with Tranio and the old man, why not rush things a little to make sure that you get the girl and she is yours forever? Take her to the church, gather about you the priest, clerk, and some honest witnesses, and do what people do at weddings. If this is not what you want, then I have no more to say except that you ought to tell Bianca farewell for forever and a day."

"Listen, Biondello —"

"I cannot tarry," Biondello said. "But I can tell you that I knew a woman who was married one afternoon as she went to the garden to get parsley to stuff a rabbit. You may do much the same thing, sir, and so goodbye, sir. My master the pretend Lucentio has ordered me to go to Saint Luke's and tell the priest to be ready to marry you when you come with the woman who will complete you."

Biondello left.

Lucentio said, "I may do this, and I will do this, if it pleases Bianca. But she will definitely be pleased, so why should I worry about what I should do?

Whatever will be will be. I will go to Bianca and ask her to marry me now. It would be embarrassing if I showed up at the church alone."

— 4.5 —

Petruchio, Katherina, Hortensio, Grumio, and some servants were traveling on the road to Padua to go to Katherina's father's house.

Katherina was thinking:

I have a decision to make. Do I allow myself to be tamed, or do I continue to resist obeying my husband, Petruchio?

Or, better, do I tame myself?

If I am tamed through the use of hunger and lack of sleep, I am no better than an animal, a hawk that a trainer tames. If I am tamed, I will obey my husband, but I will do so without love and without honoring him. He will not get the wife he wants, and I will no longer be Katherina. I will have no spirit.

If I tame myself, I do what I have decided to do. The hunger and exhaustion do not determine what I shall do, although they make it clear that I need to make a decision. If I tame myself, and if I keep the vow that I made before God, I will love, honor, and obey my husband. I will still be Katherina, and I will still have spirit.

Should I tame myself? Has being a shrew made me happy?

I have tied up and beaten my own sister because she would not tell me which of her suitors she liked best. She said that she had no preference. I did not believe her.

Is that the kind of person I want to be? Is that the kind of person God wants me to be? No.

And is that the kind of wife that Petruchio wants me to be? No.

What kind of husband do I want Petruchio to be? Do I want him to be a husband who ignores me? No. Do I want him to be the kind of husband who will tolerate a shrewish wife? No. I need a husband I can respect, a husband who has as much spirit as I have.

I have learned how shrewish behavior affects other people. It is not pleasant to witness. I have learned to consider the feelings of other people — now I have empathy for other people and do not want to see them harshly criticized for minor faults or for things that are mostly or entirely out of their control.

If anyone needs to be tamed, I do. I need to decide whether I should now tame myself.

If I tame myself, how will I benefit? I will be a better person, and most likely, I will get a better husband. Is Petruchio a bad husband? Does he always act like this?

79

Will he continue to act like this if I tame myself? I doubt it. It is obvious that he seriously takes the vow I made before God — to love, honor, and obey my husband. I think that he seriously takes the vow he made before God — to love and cherish his wife. If he had no intention of keeping his vow, he would ignore me and allow me to remain a shrew. Instead, he is going to great lengths to be married to a good wife. Also, what he does to me he is doing to himself. I am hungry, and I can look at him and see that he has lost weight. I sleep very little, and he sleeps very little so that he can ensure that I stay awake. He treats his wife as he treats himself.

But am I his wife? Are we husband and wife? Not yet. Not really. We have not consummated the marriage. I respect that in him. He is not a rapist. He will not sleep with me and consummate the marriage until I am the wife he wants and until I truly embrace a Christian marriage.

So, I have a decision to make: To be a shrew, or not to be a shrew?

Petruchio said, "So now we are on the way toward our father's house. Good Lord, how bright and goodly shines the Moon!"

Katherina said, "The Moon! It is the Sun that is shining: It is not Moonlight now."

"I say it is the Moon that shines so bright," Petruchio replied.

"I know it is the Sun that shines so bright," Katherina said.

'Now, by my mother's son, and that's myself," Petruchio said, "it shall be Moon, or Sun, or whatever I say it is before I journey to your father's house. It is time for us to turn our horses around and return home. You contradict me and contradict me and contradict me."

Hortensio said to Katherina, "Say what he wants you to say, or we shall never go to Padua."

Katherina thought, *I have made my decision.*

"Let us go forward, please, since we have come so far," Katherina said. "And let it be Moon, or Sun, or whatever you please. If you want to call it a poor and dimly lit candle, henceforth I vow it shall be so for me."

"I say it is the Moon," Petruchio said.

"I know it is the Moon," Katherina replied.

"Nay, then you lie: It is the blessed Sun."

"Then, God be blessed, it is the blessed Sun. But Sun it is not, when you say it is not. And the Moon changes even as your mind. What you will have it named, that is what it is; and so it shall be so for Katherina."

Petruchio thought, *Husbands and wives should be able to speak plainly to each other. The Moon changes from New Moon to Full Moon, and Katherina said that my mind changes like the Moon changes. Katherina knows that the Sun is the Sun. She is obeying me, but she knows what reality is and she is letting me know that she knows. Lunatics are also supposed to be adversely affected by the Moon, which is* Luna *in Latin. Katherina is implying that I am acting like a lunatic. To be honest, the things that I have been doing are things that a lunatic would do — except that I have a very good reason for doing them. Katherina is still spirited, but Katherina is a better Katherina, and I like it. And very soon I intend to stop acting like a lunatic.*

Hortensio whispered to Petruchio, "You have won. You have tamed the shrew."

Petruchio said, "Well, let us go forward, then. This is the way that things should be. The bowling ball should curve naturally and make a strike and not curve unnaturally and go into the gutter."

He thought, *Katherina is behaving as she ought to behave.*

He saw someone coming and said, "Look, we are about to have some company."

Lucentio's real father, Vincentio, walked toward them. He was an old man.

Petruchio said to him, "Good morning, young mistress. Where are you headed?"

He added, "Tell me, sweet Kate, and tell me truly, too. Have you ever seen a more youthful gentlewoman? White and red compete within her cheeks! What stars spangle Heaven with as much beauty as those two eyes that beautify her Heavenly face?"

He said to Vincentio, "Fair lovely maiden, once more good morning to you."

He added, "Sweet Kate, embrace her for her beauty's sake."

Hortensio thought, *He will make this old man mad by pretending that this old man is a young woman.*

Katherina hugged Vincentio and said, "Young budding virgin, fair and fresh and sweet, to where are you going and where do you live? Happy are the parents of so fair a child as you, and even happier will be the man to whom a happy fate will allot you to be his wife and his lovely bed-fellow!"

Petruchio thought, *Kate has out-done me. When we first met, we had a battle of wits and I narrowly defeated her. Now we are having a contest of wits — a game of wits — and she has defeated me by being funnier than me. This is the new Katherina — the spirited but faithful-to-her-marriage-vow Katherina. I have never been so happy to be defeated in my life.*

When a wife is obedient, that does not mean that she is a slave. A husband and a wife should work toward the same goals and not oppose each other. Those goals should be worthy. I admit that much of what I am requiring Katherina to do is silly, but I want that to stop soon. As soon as I know that both of us — not just me — are taking our marriage vows seriously, I will stop this silliness, and Katherina and I will work toward worthy goals.

A husband is supposed to love and cherish his wife. That means to treat her with respect and affection and tenderness. And according to 1 Peter 3:7, a husband must honor his wife: "Likewise, you husbands, dwell with them according to knowledge, giving honor to the wife, as to the weaker vessel, and as being heirs together of the grace of life; that your prayers be not hindered."

According to Proverbs 31:10, the worth of a virtuous woman is far above the worth of rubies.

He said, "Why, Kate! I hope that you are not mad. This is a man, old, wrinkled, faded, and withered. He is not a maiden, as you said he is."

"Pardon, old father, my mistaking eyes," Katherina said, "that have been so bedazzled by the Sun" — she glanced at Petruchio to see whether the Sun was still the Sun; it was — "that everything I look on seems young. Now I see that you are a reverend father. Pardon me, please, for my mad mistaking."

Katherina smiled at Petruchio, who thought, *Katherina has learned to play and to be funny.*

"Do, good old grandsire," Petruchio said, "let us know which way you are travelling. If you travel along with us, we shall be happy to have your company."

"Fair sir, and you my merry mistress, your greeting of me has much amazed me. But my name is Vincentio; I live in Pisa; and I am traveling to Padua to visit a son of mine, whom I have not seen for a long time."

"What is his name?" Petruchio asked.

"Lucentio, gentle sir."

"Then happily have we met," Petruchio said, "and happily for your son. And now by law, as well as because of your old age, I am entitled to call you my loving father. By this time, your son has married the sister of my wife, who just now greeted you, and so we are related. Do not be amazed or worried. The woman whom your son married is of good reputation, her dowry is rich, and she is of good birth. In addition, she has many good qualities that the wife of a noble gentleman ought to have. Let me hug you, and we will travel together to see your noble son, who will rejoice when you arrive."

"Is all this true?" Vincentio said. "Or is this another of the jokes that you play on travellers? You seem to enjoy playing jokes."

"I do assure you, father," Hortensio said, "that what he has said is true."

"Come with us and see for yourself that what I have said is true," Petruchio said. "I can understand that the way we first greeted you has made you wary."

Vincentio joined the travelers.

Hortensio thought, *This has been an interesting trip. I have seen how Petruchio tamed the shrew. If the widow I will soon marry turns out to be a shrew, I know exactly what to do.*

Both Petruchio and Katherina thought, *I hope that we get to Baptista's house soon — I'm starving.*

CHAPTER 5
— 5.1 —

Gremio stood in front of Lucentio's house. He did not see Biondello, Lucentio, and Bianca, who were further down the street. Lucentio was no longer disguised as Cambio.

Biondello said, "Let us move quietly and swiftly, sir; the priest is ready."

Lucentio said, "I am hurrying, Biondello, but they may need you at home so leave us and go home."

"Not yet," Biondello said. "I will go with you to the church, and then I will return to the house as quickly as I can."

Biondello, Lucentio, and Bianca left to go to the church.

"I wonder why Cambio is not here," Gremio said.

Petruchio, Katherina, Vincentio, Grumio, and some servants now arrived and went to Lucentio's house.

Petruchio said to Vincentio, "Sir, here's the door; this is Lucentio's house. My father-in-law Baptista's house is closer to the marketplace. There I must go, and so here I leave you, sir."

"You shall have a drink before you go," Vincentio said. "I think that any friend of mine will be welcomed here, and in all likelihood, some good refreshments are to be expected."

He knocked on the door.

Gremio said, "They are all busy inside; you better knock louder."

The old man who was pretending to be Vincentio looked out of a window and asked, "Who is knocking as if he would like to beat down the door?"

Vincentio asked, "Is Signior Lucentio within, sir?"

"He's inside, sir, but he is too busy to speak to anyone."

Vincentio, who had brought money to give to his son, asked, "What if a man was bringing him a hundred pounds or two, for him to spend as he wishes? Is he still too busy to talk to me?"

The old man replied, "Keep your hundred pounds to yourself: Lucentio shall not lack money as long as I live."

Petruchio said to Vincentio, "See, I told you that your son is well beloved in Padua."

Petruchio said to the old man, "Listen, sir. To make matters clear, please tell Signior Lucentio that his father has come from Pisa and is here at the door and wants to speak with him."

The old man was worried. He was pretending to be Vincentio, and here before him was the real Vincentio! He decided to continue to pretend to be Vincentio: "You lie! His father has already come from Padua and he is here and is looking out the window."

"Are you Lucentio's father?" Vincentio asked.

"Yes, sir," the old man said. "So his mother says, if I may believe her."

Petruchio said to the real Vincentio, "Why, what are you doing! This is outright knavery — you have taken another man's name and are pretending to be him."

The old man at the window said, "Lay hands on the villain and arrest him. I believe that he intends to cheat somebody in this city while pretending to be me."

Biondello arrived.

He thought, *I have seen Lucentio and Bianca in the church together. May God bless them! But who is here? He is my old master: Vincentio! Now our plans are undone and brought to ruin!*

Vincentio saw Biondello, recognized him, and said, "Come here, you rope-stretcher! Your neck was made to fit a hangman's noose!"

Biondello decided to brazen it out and said, "You are not the boss of me."

"Come here, you rogue," Vincentio said. "What, have you forgotten me?"

"Forgotten you!" Biondello replied. "No, sir. I could not forget you because I have never seen you before in all my life."

"What, you notorious villain, have you never seen your master's father, Vincentio?"

"The father of my master? Yes, indeed, sir. I see him right now — he is looking out of the window."

"Is that so!" Vincentio said. He hit Biondello.

Biondello shouted, "Help, help, help! This is a madman who wants to murder me!"

He ran away.

The old man who was pretending to be Vincentio shouted, "Help, son! Help, Signior Baptista!"

The old man withdrew from the window.

Petruchio said, "Kate, let's stay here and see what happens."

They withdrew a little to a spot where they could still see what happened.

The old man who was playing Vincentio walked onto the street. So did Tranio, Baptista, and some servants.

Tranio recognized Vincentio and decided to try to brazen it out. He said, "Sir, who are you to presume to beat my servant?"

"Who am I!" Vincentio cried. "Who are you? Oh, my God! You are a fine villain! Look at what you are wearing! A silk jacket! Velvet stockings! A scarlet cloak! And a fancy hat! The work I have done is undone! While I carefully manage my money at home, my son and my servant spend all I have at the university!"

Tranio said to Vincentio, "What's the matter with you?"

"Is this man a lunatic?" Baptista asked.

Tranio said to Vincentio, "Sir, you seem to be a respectable old gentleman judging by your clothing, but your words show that you are a madman. Why, sir, what concern is it of yours if I wear pearls and gold? I thank my good father, with whose help I am able to buy my fine clothing."

"With the help of your father!" Vincentio said. "Villain! Your father is a sail maker in Bergamo."

"You are mistaken, sir," Baptista said. "You are definitely mistaken, sir. What do you think is this man's name?"

"What is his name?" Vincentio said. "I know his name! I have brought him up ever since he was three years old, and his name is Tranio."

The old man who was pretending to be Vincentio said, "Away, away, mad ass! This man's name is Lucentio, and he is my only son and the only heir to the lands of me, Signior Vincentio."

"You think that his name is Lucentio!" Vincentio said. "Oh, he must have murdered his master! I order you in the Duke's name to lay hold of him and arrest him. Oh, my son, my son!"

He said to Tranio, "Tell me, villain, where is my son, Lucentio?"

"Bring a police officer here," Tranio ordered.

A servant arrived with a police officer, and Tranio said, "Carry this mad knave to prison. Father Baptista, we must see that this man is brought to trial."

"Carry me to prison!" Vincentio exclaimed.

Gremio said, "Wait, officer. This man shall not go to prison."

"Be quiet, Gremio," Baptista said. "I say that he shall go to prison."

"Be careful, Signior Baptista, lest you be tricked in this business," Gremio said. "I dare to swear that this man is the right Vincentio."

"Swear, if you dare," the old man pretending to be Vincentio said.

Gremio backtracked and said, "No, I dare not swear it."

"Are you willing to say that I am not Lucentio?" Tranio asked.

"No, I know that you are Lucentio," Gremio replied.

Baptista said about the real Vincentio, "Away with the dotard! Take him to prison!"

"In Padua, strangers are harassed and abused," Vincentio said. "This is monstrous!"

Biondello arrived with Lucentio and Bianca. Biondello had told them about the situation they would face.

"We are ruined and — there he is," Biondello said. "Deny that he is the real Vincentio or else we are all ruined!"

Lucentio did not deny his father.

Instead, he kneeled before him — and made Bianca also kneel — and said, "Pardon me, sweet father."

"Is my sweet son still alive?" Vincentio said. He had truly been afraid that Tranio and Biondello had murdered his son so that they could steal his identity and his money and his possessions.

Seeing and hearing this, Biondello, Tranio, and the old man who had pretended to be Vincentio ran away as quickly as they could.

Bianca said, "Pardon me, dear father."

Baptista asked her, "How have you offended me? Where is Lucentio?"

Baptista meant Tranio, who had run away, but the real Lucentio said, "Here I am. I am the real Lucentio, the real son to this man, the real Vincentio. I have married your daughter, Bianca, and have made her mine. I did that while you were blinded by counterfeits who pretended to be me and my father."

"Here is a conspiracy, with no mistake," Gremio said. "They have deceived us all!"

"Where is that damned villain Tranio?" Vincentio asked. "I have not forgotten how he badly treated and defied me."

Still puzzled, Baptista asked, "Why, is not this man Cambio?"

Bianca replied, "Cambio is really Lucentio."

"Love resulted in these miracles," Lucentio said. "My love for Bianca made me give my identity to Tranio. He became a master, and I became a servant. He pretended to be me here in Padua. But finally and happily I have arrived at the wished-for haven of my bliss by marrying Bianca. What Tranio did, I myself forced him to do, so pardon him, sweet father, for my sake."

Vincentio said, "I'll slit the villain's nose — he would have sent me to prison!"

Baptista said to Lucentio, "Listen, and answer me. Have you married my daughter without my consent?"

Vincentio replied for his son, "Do not worry, Baptista. We will make you happy with the dower we will give Bianca. Let us go inside and make everything right."

Baptista followed him inside the house, saying, "We need to get to the bottom of all this and fix it."

Lucentio said, "Don't look pale, Bianca. My father will give you a good dower, and your father will not frown at you."

Gremio said, "My attempt to be married has utterly failed, but I will go inside with everybody else. I hope to be invited to the wedding and get a share of the feast."

Katherina said, "Husband, let's follow all the others and see the end of this ado."

"First kiss me, Kate, and we will."

"What, kiss you in the middle of the street?"

Petruchio smiled and said gently, "What, are you ashamed of me?"

"No, sir, God forbid that, but I am ashamed to kiss you in the street."

"Why, then let's go home again. Come, let us leave now."

"No, I will give you a kiss."

She gave him a quick kiss and said, "Now, please, my love, let us follow the others."

"Is not this good?" Petruchio said. "Come, my sweet Kate. Better once — at some time — than never, for never is too late to mend. Better late than never, and better late than later."

In Lucentio's house, everyone was celebrating the marriage of Lucentio and Bianca. Many people were present, including Baptista, Vincentio, Gremio, Petruchio and Katherina, Hortensio and the widow he had married, Lucentio and Bianca, Biondello, and Grumio. Vincentio had decided not to severely punish Tranio, who was now bringing in dessert.

Lucentio said, "At last, though after a long time, our jarring notes are in harmony, and it is time, now that the raging war is done, to smile at escapes and dangers that have passed.

"My fair Bianca, bid my father welcome, while I with the same courtesy welcome your father.

"Brother Petruchio, sister Katherina, and you, Hortensio, with your loving widow, feast with your best appetite, and welcome to my house.

"This dessert will finish the meal that began with our great good reception at Baptista's house. Please, everyone, sit down. We now sit to chat as well as eat."

Petruchio, who had been stuffing himself — so had Katherina — said, "We do nothing but sit and sit, and eat and eat!"

Baptista said, "Padua is famous for this kind of hospitality, son Petruchio."

"Padua contains everything that is kind," Petruchio replied.

Hortensio said, "For both our sakes, I wish that word 'kind' were true."

"Now, by my life," Petruchio said, "Hortensio fears his widow. He wishes that his widow were kind."

Not quite hearing, the widow replied, "Did you say that my husband frightens me? Believe me when I say that I am not afraid of him."

"That is sensible," Petruchio said, "but you did not hear me correctly. I meant that Hortensio is afraid of you."

The widow replied, "He who is giddy thinks the world turns round."

Petruchio joked, "Roundly — that is, smartly — replied."

Katherina, however, did not like what the widow had said. If a giddy man thinks that the world turns round, then a man who is afraid of his wife thinks that other men are afraid of their wives. Why would a man be afraid of his wife? Because his wife is a shrew.

She asked the widow, "What do you mean by your comment that 'he who is giddy thinks the world turns round'?"

The widow replied, "I mean what I conceive by your husband and his comment about Hortensio."

"Conceive by Kate's husband?" Petruchio said. "Why, that is me! How do you, Hortensio, like your wife's conceiving by me? Shall you soon hear the pitter-patter of little feet?"

"My wife means that she conceived what she believes by hearing your comment," Hortensio said.

"Very well interpreted, Hortensio," Petruchio said. "Kiss him for that, good widow."

Katherina repeated, "'He who is giddy thinks the world turns round.' Please, tell me what you meant by that."

The widow, who well knew Katherina's reputation as a shrew, replied, "Your husband, being troubled with a shrew, projects his own trouble onto my husband, and now you know my meaning."

"It is a very mean — a very contemptible — meaning," Katherina said.

"Yes, it is mean," the widow said. "I mean you."

"I am mean indeed — when it comes to you," Katherina said.

"Catfight! You tell her, Kate!" Petruchio said.

"You tell her, widow!" Hortensio said.

"I bet a hundred marks that my Kate defeats the widow," Petruchio said. "My Kate will put her down."

"That's my job," Hortensio said. "I will put the widow down on her back and do what husbands do."

"That is your office, and so you are an officer," Petruchio said. "Let me drink to you."

He drank.

Baptista asked Gremio, "How do you like these quick-witted folks?"

"Believe me, sir, they like to butt their heads together."

"Head and butt!" Bianca said. "A quick-witted person would say that those butt-heads are likely to have heads with horns — cuckolds' horns.

"Ah, mistress bride," Vincentio said, "Has that awakened you?"

"Yes, it has awakened me, but it has not frightened me," Bianca replied. "Therefore, I'll go to sleep again."

"No," Petruchio said. "Don't go back to sleep. Since you have awakened and made a jest, I will target you with a shrewd jest or two of my own."

"Am I your target? Am I a bird that you are hunting?" Bianca asked. "I will move my bush and go to another bush; if you want, you can follow me and draw your bow. Please pardon me."

Bianca, Katherina, and the widow went into another room, leaving the men behind.

"She has forestalled me," Petruchio said. "Signior Tranio, Bianca is the bird you aimed at, although you did not hit her, and therefore let us drink to all who shot at her and missed."

Tranio replied, "I acted like a greyhound that Lucentio had freed from the leash. I ran after Bianca but made sure that Lucentio got the catch."

"That is a good swift simile," Petruchio said, "but something currish — pun definitely intended."

Tranio said, "It is good, sir, that you did your own hunting, but it is thought that your deer — that is, dear — holds you at bay. Does she wear the pants in your family?"

"Petruchio!" Baptista said. "Tranio got you!"

Lucentio said, "Thank you for that jest, good Tranio."

"Confess," Hortensio said. "Hasn't Tranio hit his target?"

"It is a notable quip, I agree," Petruchio said. "However, although it hit its target, it bounced off me and ten to one it hit one of you and stuck there."

"Seriously," Baptista said, "I know my daughter Katherina, and good Petruchio, I think you have the most thoroughgoing shrew of anyone here."

"Well, I say that I don't," Petruchio said. "But let's put it to the test. Let each of us send for his wife, and he whose wife is the most obedient and comes quickest when he sends for her shall win the wager that we will propose."

"Good idea," Hortensio said. "What wager will we make?"

Lucentio said, "Twenty crowns."

"Twenty crowns!" Petruchio said. "I'll venture that much on my hawk or hound, but twenty times that much on my wife."

"Make it a hundred crowns," Lucentio said.

"Agreed," Hortensio said.

"Agreed," Petruchio said. "We have made our bet."

"Who will go first?" Hortensio asked.

"I will," Lucentio replied.

He ordered, "Biondello, go to Bianca and ask her to come to me."

"I will," Biondello said, exiting.

"Son, I will assume half of your bet," Baptista said to Lucentio.

"No, I will take all the risk and all the profit for myself," Lucentio said. "I am sure that Bianca will come."

Biondello came back, alone.

"What happened?" Lucentio asked.

"Sir, my mistress sends you word that she is busy and she cannot come," Biondello replied.

Petruchio laughed and said, "What! She is busy and she cannot come! Is that the answer you were expecting?"

Gremio said, "At least it is a polite answer. You better pray to God that your own wife will not send you a worse one."

"I expect to receive a better answer," Petruchio said.

Hortensio said, "Biondello, go and entreat my wife to come to me immediately."

Petruchio said, "'Entreat'? Once she hears that, your widow must come, I suppose."

Hortensio said, "I am afraid, sir, that no matter what you do, your own wife will not come to you when asked."

Biondello came back, alone.

"Now, where's my wife?" Hortensio said.

"She says that you have some kind of practical joke in mind, and so she will not come. She told me to tell you to come to her," Biondello said.

"Worse and worse; she will not come! Oh, such a reply is vile, intolerable, and not to be endured!" Petruchio said. "Grumio, go to your mistress and tell her that I command her to come to me."

Grumio exited.

Hortensio said, "I know what your wife's answer will be."

"What?"

"She will not come."

"Then the fouler fortune is mine, and that's all there is to it."

Baptista looked up and said, "I don't believe it! Katherina is coming!"

Katherina asked Petruchio, "What may I do for you?"

"Where are your sister and Hortensio's wife?"

"They are sitting and talking by the parlor fire."

"Bring them here," Petruchio said. "If they say that they will not come, force them to come here to their husbands. Go and bring them here right away."

Katherina exited to get Bianca and the widow.

Lucentio said, "This is a wonder, if anyone wants to talk about a wonder."

"And so it is," Hortensio said. "I wonder what will be the result of it."

Petruchio said, "The result will be a peaceful and loving and quiet life. We will have a Christian marriage, based on the rightful and proper authority of and love by a husband who earns respect and obedience and honor and love from his wife. To be short, our marriage will be all that is sweet and happy. Both she and I will take our marriage vows — the same marriage vows that all Christian husbands and wives make — seriously."

"Good fortune has fallen on you, Petruchio," Baptista said. "You have won the wager, and in addition to the money that you have won from Lucentio and Hortensio, I will give you twenty thousand crowns. This is an additional dowry for an additional daughter. The old Katherina is gone. Katherina is still a spirited Katherina, but she is a better Katherina."

"I am not done yet," Petruchio said. "I will demonstrate even better than I have that I have won the wager by displaying to better advantage Katherina's new virtue and obedience. Look. She is coming now and is bringing the disobedient wives. She has made them come although they did not want to."

Katherina had Bianca and the widow each by an arm, and she led them over to their husbands.

Petruchio said, "Katherina, your hat does not flatter you. It is a mere bauble. Throw it on the floor."

Katherina threw her hat on the floor.

The widow said, "God, I hope that I never see any troubles until *after* I act silly like that!"

"Do you men call this *silly* action a wife's *duty*?" Bianca asked.

"I wish that your duty was as 'silly,'" Lucentio said. "Your conception of a wife's duty to her husband, fair Bianca, has cost me a hundred crowns since suppertime."

"The more fool you, for betting on my duty," Bianca said.

Petruchio said, "Katherina, please tell these headstrong women what duty they owe to their Lords and husbands."

"You're joking," the widow said. "We will listen to no lectures."

"Speak, Katherina," Petruchio said, "and begin with the widow. Tell her what is her duty to her husband."

"She shall not," the widow said.

"I say that she shall," Petruchio said, "and I insist that my wife begin by telling you your duty to your husband."

Katherina thought about what the Bible says about a wife's duty to her husband:

"Wives, submit yourselves unto your own husbands, as unto the Lord." — Ephesians 5:22

"For the husband is the head of the wife, even as Christ is the head of the church: and he is the savior of the body." — Ephesians 5:23

"Therefore as the church is subject unto Christ, so let the wives be [that is, submit] to their own husbands in everything." — Ephesians 5:24

She also thought about what the Bible says about a husband's duty to his wife:

"Husbands, love your wives, even as Christ also loved the church, and gave himself for it;" — Ephesians 5:25

"Likewise, you husbands, dwell with them according to knowledge, giving honor to the wife, as to the weaker vessel, and as being heirs together of the grace of life; that your prayers be not hindered." — 1 Peter 3:7

"But if any provide not for his own, and especially for those of his own house, he has denied the faith, and is worse than an infidel." — 1 Timothy 5:8

And, of course, she thought about this verse:

"Nevertheless let everyone of you in particular so love his wife even as himself; and the wife see that she reverence her husband." — Ephesians 5:33

Katherina then gave a spirited defense of Christian marriage. She said to the widow, "Shame on you! Stop scowling! Unknit that threatening unkind brow, and stop darting scornful glances from those eyes to wound your Lord, your King, your Governor — your husband! Your scowls and frowns blot your beauty as frosts do stain the meadows. They destroy your reputation the way that whirlwinds shake fair buds, and in no sense are your scowls and frowns appropriate or amiable."

Then Katherina began to talk to both the widow and Bianca:

"An ill-tempered woman is like a troubled and agitated fountain: muddy, ill-seeming, thick, and robbed of beauty. And while the fountain is like that, no one — no matter how dry or thirsty he is — will deign to sip or touch one drop of it.

"Your husband is your Lord, your life, your keeper, your head, your King; he is the one who cares for you, and to be able to take good care of you he commits his body to painful labor both by sea and land. He stays awake during storms at sea and during cold weather by day while you are lying warm at home, secure and safe. Your husband craves no other tribute at your hands but love, fair looks, and true obedience; this is too little payment for so great a debt.

"Such duty as the subject owes the Prince is what a wife owes to her husband, and when she is perverse, peevish, sullen, sour, and not obedient to his honest and honorable will, what is she but a foul and willful rebel and graceless traitor to her loving Lord?

"I am ashamed that women are so simple-minded as to offer war when and where they should kneel for peace — or to seek for rule, supremacy, and sway, when they are bound to serve, love, and obey.

"Why are our bodies made so soft and weak and smooth, unfitted to toil and trouble in the world, except for the reason that our soft conditions and our hearts should well agree with our external parts?

"Come, you perverse and incapable worms — you disobedient wives! My mind has been as big and proud as one of yours. My courage has been as great, and my intelligence and character perhaps even more suited than yours to shoot forth insulting words and shoot forth frowns. But now I see that our lances are only straws. Our strength is weak, and our weakness is past comparison. When wives wear the pants in the family, wives are at their worst and weakest.

"So suppress your pride, which is of no use to you. Metaphorically place your hands below your husband's foot. To show my husband that I am loyal to him, I am willing to do that literally as well as metaphorically, if he should ever want me to."

"Why, there's a wife!" Petruchio said. "Come on, and kiss me, Kate."

They kissed for real, lips on lips.

Lucentio said, "Well done and congratulations, old pal. You have won the bet, and you have won a good wife."

Vincentio said, "It is good news when one's children are well behaved and obedient."

Lucentio said glumly, "But it is bad news when women and wives are badly behaved and disobedient."

"Come, Kate, we will go to bed," Petruchio said. "We three couples are all married, but I predict that two of the marriages will have problems."

He said to Lucentio, who had married Bianca, whose name means white, "It was I who won the wager, though you won the white. Now that I am a winner, may God give you a good night!"

Petruchio and Katherina left to consummate their marriage.

Hortensio said, "Well, Petruchio, run along. You have tamed a curst shrew."

Lucentio said, "It is a wonder, if you don't mind my saying so, that she allowed herself to be tamed."

AFTERWORD

As he took his bows at the end of the play, the actor playing Christopher Sly thought, *I am glad that this is a play. Obviously, we can learn about Christian marriage from this play, but anyone who wants to do in real life what Petruchio does in this play is a complete and utter idiot.*

In writing the above paragraph, I do not think that I am going against Shakespeare. I believe that the major purpose of the Christopher Sly introduction is to strongly tell the audience that *The Taming of the Shrew* is a play. What better way to emphasize that than to make *The Taming of the Shrew* a play within a play? The appearance of the actor playing Christopher Sly during the curtain call is another strong reminder that *The Taming of the Shrew* is a play. When the actor playing Christopher Sly appears during the curtain call, the male audience members should be thinking, "I have just seen a theatrical comedy. I better not try to imitate Petruchio at home!"

By the way, according to Wikipedia ("Marriage Vows"), "On September 12, 1922, the Episcopal Church voted to remove the word 'obey' from the bride's section of wedding vows."

APPENDIX A: ABOUT THE AUTHOR

It was a dark and stormy night. Suddenly a cry rang out, and on a hot summer night in 1954, Josephine, wife of Carl Bruce, gave birth to a boy — me. Unfortunately, this young married couple allowed Reuben Saturday, Josephine's brother, to name their first-born. Reuben, aka "The Joker," decided that Bruce was a nice name, so he decided to name me Bruce Bruce. I have gone by my middle name — David — ever since.

Being named Bruce David Bruce hasn't been all bad. Bank tellers remember me very quickly, so I don't often have to show an ID. It can be fun in charades, also. When I was a counselor as a teenager at Camp Echoing Hills in Warsaw, Ohio, a fellow counselor gave the signs for "sounds like" and "two words," then she pointed to a bruise on her leg twice. Bruise Bruise? Oh yeah, Bruce Bruce is the answer!

Uncle Reuben, by the way, gave me a haircut when I was in kindergarten. He cut my hair short and shaved a small bald spot on the back of my head. My mother wouldn't let me go to school until the bald spot grew out again.

Of all my brothers and sisters (six in all), I am the only transplant to Athens, Ohio. I was born in Newark, Ohio, and have lived all around Southeastern Ohio. However, I moved to Athens to go to Ohio University and have never left.

At Ohio U, I never could make up my mind whether to major in English or Philosophy, so I got a bachelor's degree with a double major in both areas, then I added a master's degree in English and a master's degree in Philosophy.

Currently, and for a long time to come (I eat fruits and vegetables), I am spending my retirement writing books such as *Nadia Comaneci: Perfect 10*, *The Funniest People in Dance*, *Homer's* Iliad: *A Retelling in Prose*, and *William Shakespeare's* Macbeth: *A Retelling in Prose*.

By the way, my sister Brenda Kennedy writes romances such as *A New Beginning* and *Shattered Dreams*.

APPENDIX B: SOME BOOKS BY DAVID BRUCE

Retellings of a Classic Work of Literature

Arden of Faversham: A Retelling

Ben Jonson's The Alchemist: *A Retelling*

Ben Jonson's The Arraignment, or Poetaster: *A Retelling*

Ben Jonson's Bartholomew Fair: *A Retelling*

Ben Jonson's The Case is Altered: *A Retelling*

Ben Jonson's Catiline's Conspiracy: *A Retelling*

Ben Jonson's The Devil is an Ass: *A Retelling*

Ben Jonson's Epicene: *A Retelling*

Ben Jonson's Every Man in His Humor: *A Retelling*

Ben Jonson's Every Man Out of His Humor: *A Retelling*

Ben Jonson's The Fountain of Self-Love, or Cynthia's Revels: *A Retelling*

Ben Jonson's The Magnetic Lady, or Humors Reconciled: *A Retelling*

Ben Jonson's The New Inn, or The Light Heart: *A Retelling*

Ben Jonson's Sejanus' Fall: *A Retelling*

Ben Jonson's The Staple of News: *A Retelling*

Ben Jonson's A Tale of a Tub: *A Retelling*

Ben Jonson's Volpone, or the Fox: *A Retelling*

Christopher Marlowe's Complete Plays: Retellings

Christopher Marlowe's Dido, Queen of Carthage: *A Retelling*

Christopher Marlowe's Doctor Faustus: *Retellings of the 1604 A-Text and of the 1616 B-Text*

Christopher Marlowe's Edward II: *A Retelling*

Christopher Marlowe's The Massacre at Paris: *A Retelling*

Christopher Marlowe's The Rich Jew of Malta: *A Retelling*

Christopher Marlowe's Tamburlaine, Parts 1 and 2: *Retellings*

Dante's Divine Comedy: *A Retelling in Prose*

Dante's Inferno: *A Retelling in Prose*

Dante's Purgatory: *A Retelling in Prose*

Dante's Paradise: *A Retelling in Prose*

The Famous Victories of Henry V: *A Retelling*

From the Iliad *to the* Odyssey: *A Retelling in Prose of Quintus of Smyrna's* Posthomerica

George Chapman, Ben Jonson, and John Marston's Eastward Ho! *A Retelling*

George Peele's The Arraignment of Paris: *A Retelling*

George Peele's The Battle of Alcazar: *A Retelling*

George's Peele's David and Bathsheba, and the Tragedy of Absalom: *A Retelling*

George Peele's Edward I: *A Retelling*

George Peele's The Old Wives' Tale: *A Retelling*

George-a-Greene: *A Retelling*

The History of King Leir: *A Retelling*

Homer's Iliad: *A Retelling in Prose*

Homer's Odyssey: *A Retelling in Prose*

J.W. Gent.'s The Valiant Scot: *A Retelling*

Jason and the Argonauts: A Retelling in Prose of Apollonius of Rhodes' Argonautica

John Ford: Eight Plays Translated into Modern English

John Ford's The Broken Heart: *A Retelling*

John Ford's The Fancies, Chaste and Noble: *A Retelling*

John Ford's The Lady's Trial: *A Retelling*

John Ford's The Lover's Melancholy: *A Retelling*

John Ford's Love's Sacrifice: *A Retelling*

John Ford's Perkin Warbeck: *A Retelling*

John Ford's The Queen: *A Retelling*

John Ford's 'Tis Pity She's a Whore: *A Retelling*

John Lyly's Campaspe: *A Retelling*

John Lyly's Endymion, The Man in the Moon: *A Retelling*

John Lyly's Galatea: *A Retelling*

John Lyly's Love's Metamorphosis: *A Retelling*

John Lyly's Midas: *A Retelling*

John Lyly's Mother Bombie: *A Retelling*

John Lyly's Sappho and Phao: *A Retelling*

John Lyly's The Woman in the Moon: *A Retelling*

John Webster's The White Devil: *A Retelling*

King Edward III: *A Retelling*

Mankind: *A Medieval Morality Play* (A Retelling)

Margaret Cavendish's The Unnatural Tragedy: *A Retelling*

The Merry Devil of Edmonton: *A Retelling*

The Summoning of Everyman: *A Medieval Morality Play* (A Retelling)

Robert Greene's Friar Bacon and Friar Bungay: *A Retelling*

The Taming of a Shrew: *A Retelling*

Tarlton's Jests: A Retelling

Thomas Middleton's A Chaste Maid in Cheapside: *A Retelling*

Thomas Middleton's Women Beware Women: *A Retelling*

Thomas Middleton and Thomas Dekker's The Roaring Girl: *A Retelling*

Thomas Middleton and William Rowley's The Changeling: *A Retelling*

The Trojan War and Its Aftermath: Four Ancient Epic Poems

Virgil's Aeneid: *A Retelling in Prose*

William Shakespeare's 5 Late Romances: Retellings in Prose

William Shakespeare's 10 Histories: Retellings in Prose

William Shakespeare's 11 Tragedies: Retellings in Prose

William Shakespeare's 12 Comedies: Retellings in Prose

William Shakespeare's 38 Plays: Retellings in Prose

William Shakespeare's 1 Henry IV, aka Henry IV, Part 1: *A Retelling in Prose*

William Shakespeare's 2 Henry IV, aka Henry IV, Part 2: *A Retelling in Prose*

William Shakespeare's 1 Henry VI, aka Henry VI, Part 1: *A Retelling in Prose*

William Shakespeare's 2 Henry VI, aka Henry VI, Part 2: *A Retelling in Prose*

William Shakespeare's 3 Henry VI, aka Henry VI, Part 3: *A Retelling in Prose*

William Shakespeare's All's Well that Ends Well: *A Retelling in Prose*

William Shakespeare's Antony and Cleopatra: *A Retelling in Prose*

William Shakespeare's As You Like It: *A Retelling in Prose*

William Shakespeare's The Comedy of Errors: *A Retelling in Prose*

William Shakespeare's Coriolanus: *A Retelling in Prose*

William Shakespeare's Cymbeline: *A Retelling in Prose*

William Shakespeare's Hamlet: *A Retelling in Prose*

William Shakespeare's Henry V: *A Retelling in Prose*

William Shakespeare's Henry VIII: *A Retelling in Prose*

William Shakespeare's Julius Caesar: *A Retelling in Prose*

William Shakespeare's King John: *A Retelling in Prose*

William Shakespeare's King Lear: *A Retelling in Prose*

William Shakespeare's Love's Labor's Lost: *A Retelling in Prose*

William Shakespeare's Macbeth: *A Retelling in Prose*

William Shakespeare's Measure for Measure: *A Retelling in Prose*

William Shakespeare's The Merchant of Venice: *A Retelling in Prose*

William Shakespeare's The Merry Wives of Windsor: *A Retelling in Prose*

William Shakespeare's A Midsummer Night's Dream: *A Retelling in Prose*

William Shakespeare's Much Ado About Nothing: *A Retelling in Prose*

William Shakespeare's Othello: *A Retelling in Prose*

William Shakespeare's Pericles, Prince of Tyre: *A Retelling in Prose*

William Shakespeare's Richard II: *A Retelling in Prose*

William Shakespeare's Richard III: *A Retelling in Prose*

William Shakespeare's Romeo and Juliet: *A Retelling in Prose*

William Shakespeare's The Taming of the Shrew: *A Retelling in Prose*

William Shakespeare's The Tempest: *A Retelling in Prose*

William Shakespeare's Timon of Athens: *A Retelling in Prose*

William Shakespeare's Titus Andronicus: *A Retelling in Prose*

William Shakespeare's Troilus and Cressida: *A Retelling in Prose*

William Shakespeare's Twelfth Night: *A Retelling in Prose*

William Shakespeare's The Two Gentlemen of Verona: *A Retelling in Prose*

William Shakespeare's The Two Noble Kinsmen: *A Retelling in Prose*

William Shakespeare's The Winter's Tale: *A Retelling in Prose*